ACCORDING TO CRITICS,

# AN ARMY OF FROGS

KICKS SOME SERIOUS SCORPION BUTT!

"This little frog should find fans among readers
of the Warriors and Redwall sagas."

—KIRKUS REVIEWS

"The violent but not overly graphic action
is well matched by Greene's dynamic
and plentiful full-color illustrations."

—BOOKLIST

"A must-have, winning adventure
that is nearly impossible to put down."

—SCHOOL LIBRARY JOURNAL

"Greene's color full-page illustrations have the
richly saturated look of Marvel comic books."

—BULLETIN OF THE CENTER FOR CHILDREN'S BOOKS

"This clever fantasy series featuring frogs
versus scorpions, set in Australia,
makes for pleasant reading."

—LIBRARY MEDIA CONNECTION

BY TREVOR PRYCE WITH JOEL NAFTALI

ILLUSTRATED BY SANFORD GREENE

AMULET BOOKS
NEW YORK

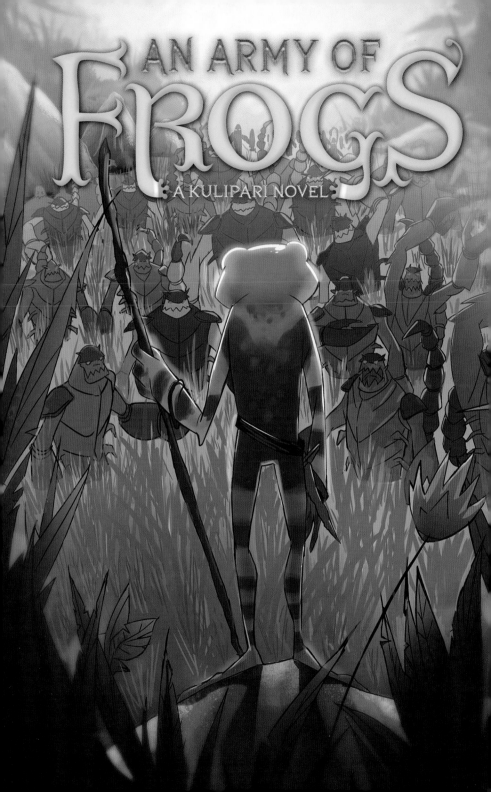

The Library of Congress has catalogued the hardcover edition of this
book as follows:
Pryce, Trevor.
An army of frogs : a Kulipari novel / Trevor Pryce with Joel Naftali.
p.cm.
ISBN 978-1-4197-0172-6
[1. Frogs—Fiction. 2. Magic—Fiction. 3. Spiders—Fiction.
4. Scorpions—Fiction. 5. Fantasy—Fiction.] I. Naftali, Joel. II. Title.
PZ7.P9493496 Arm 2013
[Fic]—dc23
2012027726

ISBN for this edition: 978-1-4197-1381-1

Text copyright © 2013 Trevor Pryce
Illustrations copyright © 2013 Sanford Greene
Book design by Sara Corbett

Amulet Books and Amulet Paperbacks are registered trademarks of
Harry N. Abrams, Inc.

Printed in China
10 9 8 7 6 5 4 3 2 1

Amulet Books are available at special discounts when purchased in
quantity for premiums and promotions as well as fund-raising or
educational use. Special editions can also be created to specification.
For details, contact specialsales@abramsbooks.com
or the address below.

ABRAMS
THE ART OF BOOKS SINCE 1949
115 West 18th Street
New York, NY 10011
www.abramsbooks.com

TO SONYA AND THE KIDS.
LOVE YOU ALL DEARLY AND THANK
YOU FOR THE SUPPORT. —T.P.

FOR BZ. —J.N.

TO MY WIFE, LESLI,
WHO MEANS THE WORLD TO ME.
TO MY SONS, MALCOLM AND MASON,
FOR BEING THE PERFECT FOCUS GROUP.
AND TO GOD FOR ALLOWING ME
TO USE MY TALENTS. —S.G.

DAREL

GURNUGAN (GEE)
DAREL'S BEST FRIEND

GEE'S MOTHER
AND FATHER

THUMA

DAREL'S MOTHER
A WOOD FROG

THARTA

OLD JIR
A FORMER KULIPARI

MIRO
GEE'S LITTLE
BROTHER

DAREL'S YOUNGER
TRIPLET SIBLINGS

ARABANOO

TIPI

ARABANOO'S
GANG

GANG LEADER AND
NEMESIS OF DAREL

FROGS AND TURTLES

VERSUS

LORD MARMOO
LEADER OF THE SCORPIONS

COMMANDER PIGO

LORD MARMOO'S
SECOND-IN-COMMAND

THREE-TOED
SKINK MERCENARY

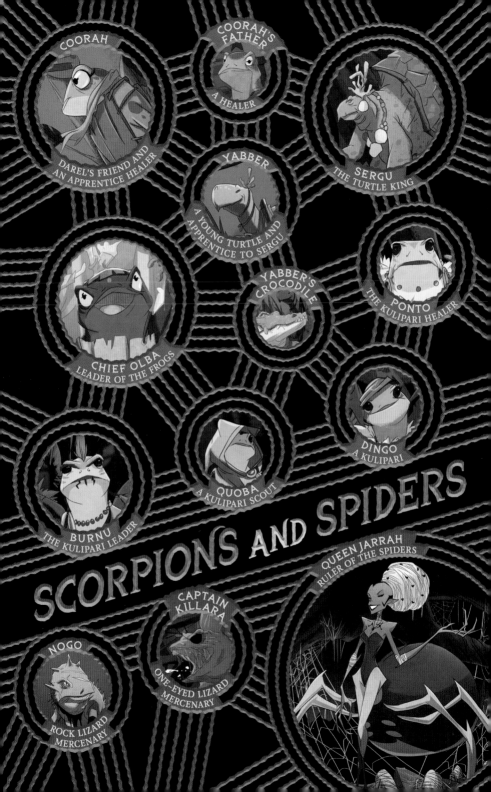

# 1

WITH THE STEALTH OF A warrior, Darel hopped along a wide branch, tracking the two scouts below. A waterfall roared in the distance, and a tasty-looking fig wasp flitted past. Darel ignored a pang of hunger, resisting the urge to shoot his tongue at the wasp for a quick snack.

Dinner could wait until he'd dealt with the enemy.

The banyan tree rose a hundred feet above Darel, into the wide Australian sky, and was anchored to the earth by dozens of ropy-looking roots. The warm glow of sunset filtered through the leaves and dappled the ground beside the two scouts.

They crept past the dark mouths of burrows, then stopped. The stout one scanned the roots of the banyan. The smaller one glanced around nervously, alert to every fluttering leaf and chirping insect.

Invisible to the enemy, Darel clung to the side of the branch with his finger pads. He touched the handle of his dagger for good luck, then leaped from the tree. He landed on a lichen-spotted boulder above the path, his blood thrilling to the hunt.

He grabbed a nearby stick and, with a low growl, sprang at the scouts.

The smaller scout screamed, but the stout one thrust with his stick, his yellow eyes determined.

Darel parried the blow, and the two sticks met with a loud *thuk*. "Back to the desert, scorpion!" he cried.

"Surrender, croaker," the stout one sneered, "or I'll—" He dodged wildly when the knobby end of Darel's stick whizzed toward him.

"Or you'll *what*?" Darel asked. He jammed his stick into the forest floor and pole-vaulted over the enemy, twisting in the air to smack him from above.

It was a beautiful acrobatic move, except his stick slipped and he crashed to the ground.

"Ha!" the scout croaked, and chopped at him with his stick.

Darel rolled away, scrambled to his feet, and lunged. His thrust missed by a mile, but that was only a feint, and his powerful kick sent the scout hurtling toward a rain puddle, where he collapsed in a moaning heap.

With a twirl of his stick, Darel turned and crouched, ready to strike the smaller scout.

"If you hit me, I'll tell Coorah!" the small frog blurted, his eyes bulging.

Darel chuckled and relaxed, tossing the stick aside. "Don't worry, tadpole. What're you doing here, anyway?"

"Playing with Gee," the young frogling said, looking toward the pudgy frog in the puddle—Darel's best friend, Gurnugan.

"He's tagging along," Gurnugan said, rubbing his bruised stomach. "He's my little brother, after all."

"Maybe he'll learn something, Gee," Darel said, tossing his best friend a honey snail from his pouch.

"Yeah." Gee caught the snail with his tongue. "He'll learn that instead of going to the swimming hole with the other frogs, you spend every day practicing to be a warrior."

"Not *every* day."

"And you make your best friend play the scorpion." Gee sighed. "Plus, you hit me in the belly again."

"Well, that's a scorpion's only weak spot."

"It's not *mine*."

Darel grinned. "No, yours is pretty well padded."

"Very funny."

"Anyway, you know you love sparring."

"*You* love sparring! *I* love honey snails. Got any more?"

"Not for you," Darel said, patting his pouch. "And how're we going to become better warriors if we don't keep practicing?"

"I'm good enough, Darel. It's not like the scorpions are going to come marching into the Amphibilands. They don't even know where we are." Gee cocked his head. "Speaking of which, where were *you*? You came out of nowhere."

"The banyan tree." Darel pointed his thumb upward. "You didn't look high enough."

"The *tree*? Come here." Gee tugged Darel to the puddle's edge. "Look in the water. What do you see?"

"Um, us?"

"Us," Gee agreed. "Two ordinary wood frogs. You are *not* a tree frog."

"Never said I was. I just—"

"You know what color that is?" Gurnugan asked, pointing at Darel's reflection.

"A sort of noble green?"

"A sort of *muddy* green, Darel. Mostly brown. You are not going to grow up and become a tree frog."

"I don't want to be a tree frog."

Gee sighed and looked at his little brother. "Three guesses, Miro. What does Darel want to be when he grows up?"

The small frog blinked his inner eyelids thoughtfully. "A hunter?"

"Not a hunter."

"A diver?"

"Not a diver. This is Darel we're talking about. Think *crazy*."

"Oh, I know! A wombat!"

Gee furrowed his brow. "No, you tadpole, not a wombat."

"A platypus?"

"That's four guesses. And no, not a platypus. He wants to be"—Gurnugan waved one chubby foreleg—"a *Kulipari*."

Miro giggled. "He can't be a Kulipari!"

"Why not?" Darel demanded. "My father was a Kulipari. He was a unit leader. He was a hero."

"And he was a corroboree frog," Gurnugan said, "the only frog in the world that can produce its own poison. But you take after your mother. You're a wood frog, through and through."

"Take that back!" Darel said, glaring at him.

"I'm sorry," Gee said, raising his hands. "But . . . look at you."

"Looks can be deceiving."

"You think you're a Kulipari on the inside? Are you poisonous?"

Darel's shoulders slumped. "You know I'm not."

"Well, there you go, then." Gee turned to his little brother. "That's where the Kulipari's power comes from—poison. When they tap into their poison, their eyes turn black and their skin glows, and they can do impossible things. At least, that's what the stories say."

"I've seen it," Darel said. "When I was a tadpole, my father showed me."

Miro's eyes bulged. "Is it true that one Kulipari can beat a hundred scorpions?"

"They move so fast," Darel told him, "they're only a blur. They're strong as a falling tree and tough as packed mud. You see this dagger?" He touched a finger pad to the dagger at his side.

Miro nodded.

"It was my father's. He could throw it from here to the pond and shave the whiskers off a dragonfly."

"Dragonflies don't have whiskers," Gee said.

"They did before my dad got to 'em!"

They laughed. Then Gee shot Darel a worried look. "But, buddy? You're a wood frog; there's no poison in you. And you know what wood frogs are good for?"

"Working," little Miro said. "Even *I* know that. And working and working and working . . ."

A pinecone blurred past them, missing Darel by a toe pad's width.

# 2

IN A MUD-COLORED FLASH, DAREL LEAPED through the air and landed on a tree stump across the clearing. "Coorah!" he shouted.

A lean figure hopped onto the path, laughing softly. She was slender and graceful. She was also a wood frog, but her skin glowed bronze in the evening light, and her eyes glinted with a combination of mischief and wisdom.

"Caught you off guard, lazybones," Coorah said, fingering another pinecone. "That means you owe me a wattleflower!"

"You and your herbs—" Darel began.

"And if I *hit* you," she continued, "you promised to bring me three!"

Darel charged at Coorah, croaking his war cry, and she threw her second pinecone.

Coorah's father was the best healer in the village, and everyone expected that one day she'd be even better. But that meant she spent all her time experimenting with new medicines instead of practicing how to throw things at moving targets. She missed Darel by three feet.

Darel puffed his throat in triumph as he stalked toward her. "Surrender! Only one flower for you!"

With a teasing light in her eyes, Coorah crooked her finger at him as she leaned against the stem of a leafy plant.

Darel approached warily. Coorah was the only other frog who believed that the scorps and spiders might attack again—even Gee went along mostly to humor Darel. Coorah was a healer, though, not a fighter, so her preparation for the upcoming invasion involved finding new herbs and inventing new treatments.

But she was clever, too. Tricky.

So he didn't rush forward. Instead, he carefully hopped closer . . .

Until Coorah gave the stem beside her a quick shake. A dozen overripe figs, which were balanced on the leaves above, fell in a rain around Darel—except the one that landed on his head and burst open.

Gee and Miro laughed, but Darel continued forward, fig pulp dripping down his cheek. A true warrior was not distracted by such things.

"I surrender," Coorah said, biting her lip to keep from laughing. "You are definitely the mightiest warrior in all the Amphibilands." She paused for a second. "Or at least the stickiest."

"In the old days, before the Kulipari left," Darel said loftily, "warriors were shown some respect!"

"Even wood frog warriors with less poison than a boiled macadamia nut?" Coorah teased. "Who offer their friends wattleflowers to sneak-attack them?"

"How else am I going to learn?" Darel grumbled. He felt foolish, because she and Gee were right; he was a wood frog playing war—he wasn't a *real* soldier, despite all his grandiose daydreams.

Coorah must've heard the self-doubt in his tone. She brushed a chunk of fig from his shoulder.

"At least you're actually getting better," she said. "I'm still trying to figure out how to treat war wounds with lily pollen, and my dad just wants me to make tea for tummyaches."

"Yeah, but your grandmother said you're a natural," Darel told her. "You've got a gift for battle-field healing."

"I guess," she said, her eyes troubled. "Sometimes I think I'm just wasting my time."

Miro hopped closer and took Coorah's webbed

hand. "Can we go back now?" He glanced at his big brother. "Mom and Dad want us home, Gurnugan. If we're too late, we'll get ponded."

Gee just shrugged, even though he hated the thought of having to stay inside for a week.

Darel knew Gee would do whatever he did. Gee always backed him up, even if it meant a punishment later. He didn't like fighting, but he practiced with Darel almost every day. He didn't like stalking the older frogs in the village to hone his tracking skills, or leaping from the highest leaves of the banyan to the branches below, or bodysurfing down the rapids.

Gee didn't like doing things that no self-respecting wood frog would dream of doing. But he did them, so Darel wouldn't have to do them alone.

Darel sighed. He'd rather stay outside under the half-moon with the nocturnal frogs, practicing his climbing and burrowing and head-butting—though wood frogs didn't climb or burrow or head-butt.

But he couldn't keep dragging Gee into trouble. Gee hated getting scolded. And he hated getting head-butted, too.

Besides, Darel didn't want to disappoint his mother. Not that she ever complained. She knew her son, knew that the one thing he wanted most in the world was to follow in his father's and grandfather's footsteps. They'd both been unit leaders in the Kulipari. They'd both fought in legendary battles, and his father had died to keep the Amphibilands safe and hidden inside the Veil.

Except Darel didn't have poison—he didn't have a single drop of his father's power. He might become a *warrior* without poison, but he'd never become a *Kulipari*.

And yet . . . he couldn't stop trying. Because instead of his father's poison, he'd inherited his mother's stubborn determination.

She outhustled any other two frogs in Australia. She worked long days in her fly shop, and then, after the shop closed, she took food to the old frogs, helped any neighbors who needed assistance, and raised the triplets—Darel's siblings, who were still in the tadpool nursery.

Yet, when he came home scraped from rumbling with the white-lipped frogs or aching from bodysurfing the rapids, she'd just say, "You're your father's son."

He'd sigh. "I'm yours, too."

"And *that* is why you should know better." Then she'd kiss him on the forehead and patch him up.

She never complained, but a true Kulipari did

not shirk his duty, so Darel nodded to Gee, and they joined Coorah and Miro. They followed the river past pale green munumula trees with their long, weepy branches, hopping slowly to match the younger frog's short-legged leaps.

"When'd you put those figs there?" Darel asked Coorah, shooting out his tongue to snag bits of the fruit from his arm.

Coorah grinned. "I didn't. I just saw them and decided to lure you into a trap."

"Next time," Darel said, hopping with her through the grass hummocks, "bait it with barbecued flies. I'm starving."

"Your pouch is full of honey snails! And it's bad enough that you make Gurnugan be the scorpion every time. You think I'm going to start setting traps for you like a spider?"

"You're evil enough," Darel said, then dodged her sharp elbow.

"Um, guys?" Gee said.

"You're probably a nightcaster, too," Darel continued. "Weaving deadly spells in your malevolent web."

"'*Malevolent*'?" Coorah said. "You don't even know what that means."

"Um, guys?" Gee said again.

"I do too!" Darel told Coorah. "It means 'evil.'"

"Guys!" Gee's nostrils narrowed. "Speaking of evil . . ."

They stopped and looked at him. His yellow eyes bulged with worry, staring toward the outskirts of their village.

"I think we now know whose figs those were," he said.

# 3

 AREL PEERED INTO THE GLOOM of the evening and saw a half dozen frogs waiting in a tangle of vines that protected the village's worm farm. They were white-lipped tree frogs, the world's largest—they called themselves "Great Tree Frogs." Their slitted eyes and protuberant lower lips gave them a sulky look.

They jumped from the shadows, led by a frog named Arabanoo, who was tossing a rotten fig in one hand. He eyed Darel. The other members of his gang, three brawny girl frogs and two slightly smaller boys, glowered beside him. Each held a gross-looking fig.

"Don't you dare throw those," Coorah said, as the gang came closer. "Or I'll sprinkle itching powder in your beds."

"There's nothing we don't dare," Arabanoo told her. "We're not mud-bellies."

"That's true," Darel said. "You're sap-lickers."

"Don't you two start!" Coorah snapped. "Go pick on someone your own size, Arabanoo."

"Gurnugan *is* my size," he said, inflating his throat pouch. "At least, he's my *weight.*"

"He'd be your height, too," another white-lipped frog said, "if he was lying on his back!"

"Where do you think you're going?" Arabanoo demanded of Darel, as he moved to hop around them.

"Where do you think? The village."

Everyone called it that—*the* village—even though there were dozens of villages in the valley.

Some of the villages were in the canopies of interwoven trees, and others were in deep burrows carpeted with moss and illuminated by glowworms. There were swamp villages with reed huts, floating pond villages, and creek and grass and waterfall villages. There were even some frogs who lived in the coastal scrub, near the beach, and mostly ate crabs.

The most common, though, were the leaf villages, for ordinary wood frogs like Darel. And he didn't like to admit it, but the leaf villages were his favorite. Fallen leaves of every shape and color and size were joined to wooden frames and stone foundations, into entryways and cottages and peaks and pagodas. With bustling marketplaces and wide, smooth trails, the leaf villages were the threads that stitched the Amphibilands together.

And Darel always thought that *the* village, the capital village where the chief worked and the council met, was basically a leaf village. Most families lived in leaf huts near the riverbank, and most of the shops were leafy stalls, even though tree frogs also lived in the branching heights, swamp frogs in the marsh, and burrowers in underground caverns.

Every kind of frog lived in the village. That's what made it *the* village.

Darel took a breath and—trying to get along—quietly added, "I'm just heading home."

"Gonna wear an apron and help your mommy?" Arabanoo asked with a smirk.

"That's right," Darel said. "We weren't *all* born useless."

So much for getting along.

"Can we go now?" Miro whimpered, tugging on Coorah's hand.

"No way," she told him. "What if these wart-heads manage to really hurt each other?"

Miro's eyes bulged. "Um, I guess that would be bad."

"Are you kidding? That would be *great*. I could finally practice on real wounds."

"P-p-please can we go?"

Coorah sighed and flicked her inner eyelids. "Fine. I guess if I want to listen to a couple of tadpoles bickering, I'll visit the nursery."

She pushed through the gang, but when Darel and Gee started to follow her, Arabanoo murmured, "Is the little wood frog running away?"

Darel stopped and held the gang leader's gaze. A moment later, Gee sighed, and then he stopped, too.

"Don't forget, Darel," Coorah croaked from ahead. "You promised the chief you wouldn't fight them again."

"I'm not going to fight them."

"Of course he won't," Arabanoo said. "He doesn't want to lose again."

"It was six against one," Darel said, "and I almost won—"

"Don't let him bait you," Coorah called, leading Miro away. "You're not a sandpaper frog."

Darel nodded. Sandpaper frogs didn't live in the Amphibilands. They weren't welcome, because as tadpoles they sometimes ate their younger brothers and sisters. Not too surprisingly, many of them became mercenaries, like the lizards. They were quick to fight, and they fought for anyone who paid them. Even scorpions.

People in the village sometimes muttered that Darel should join the sandpapers because he loved sparring. He hated it when they said that. And he knew, watching Coorah turn toward the stone bridge, that she was right. He wasn't a sandpaper—he was better than that.

"I don't want to fight you," he told the white-lipped frogs.

Beside him, Gee snorted faintly.

"I *don't*," Darel said. "I just want to say, teasing a frog in front of his little brother is pretty low, Arabanoo—even for you."

A flicker of regret crossed the gang leader's face, but he stuck his white lower lip out and said, "And stealing figs is low for you."

"I didn't steal them."

"Then who did? They're gone, aren't they?"

"Yeah, but we didn't steal them, we just . . . They fell."

"You ruined them."

"I ruined your rotten figs?"

"I'm glad we agree," Arabanoo sniffed. "Now, what's in your pouch? Honey snails? We'll take them and call it even."

"I don't think so." Darel put his hand on his pouch. "Let's go, Gee."

But the second biggest of the white-lipped frogs blocked the road. "Don't make us rough you up," she growled, ". . . sandpaper boy."

## 4

AREL EYED THE PATH BEHIND the white-lipped frogs. He could leap over these jokers and be halfway to the village before they even turned around.

Except leaping wasn't really Gee's strength. Loyalty, friendship, honesty, and sheer goodness? Yes. Leaping? No.

"How about this," he said. "You let us—"

Before he could finish, a rotten fig flew through the air and smashed against Gee's chest.

"Can we just give them the snails?" Gee pleaded.

"I can't," Darel said, shaking his head.

Four more figs flew through the air and burst against Gee. He stumbled backward and fell in the dirt, covered with pieces of pulpy fig.

Darel had been taught that real warriors didn't fight unless *they* chose to. He'd been taught that real warriors did not lose their tempers and never went back on their word. And he'd given the chief his word that he wouldn't fight the white-lips, not after their last brawl had come too close to the nursery.

But he also knew that friends stood up for friends. And before he knew anything else, he felt himself shoving one of the gang members. He jumped into the air and kicked two more. Then he faced Arabanoo, and the other white-lips rushed him from behind.

He leaped away, but one of them got a finger pad on his foot and he cartwheeled in the air and came crashing down. An instant later, Arabanoo landed on his stomach with all his weight.

Darel gasped and wriggled, but three of the white-lips held him down.

Arabanoo butted him with his big bony head, and Darel saw stars. It looked like he was going to almost win another fight—which was exactly the same as losing.

Then a brown cannonball smashed into the three frogs holding him down.

Gurnugan.

He slammed the bigger frogs away from Darel, sent them sprawling to the ground. And in a moment, Darel and Gee were back-to-back, with the six big white-lips circling them angrily. It sort of reminded Darel of his daydreams about battling the scorpion horde—completely outnumbered, but guaranteed to win.

"There's six of them and two of us," Gee muttered to Darel. "And they're twice our size. So would you please stop that?"

"Stop what?"

"Stop *smiling*."

Then, on a signal from Arabanoo, the white-lips jumped them.

As night fell, they brawled past the mud flats skirting the village and wrestled beside a fallen tree, where two gang members smacked their heads against the hanging roots and sat stunned.

A shove from one of the white-lips pushed Gee into the stream. He sprawled in the shallows, moaning softly and absorbing the water through his skin to soothe himself.

Finally, Darel faced Arabanoo and his remaining followers on the top of the hill overlooking the market-place. The hill was where the peddlers stored their wares.

All the young frogs were scuffed and breathless. Only Darel and Arabanoo had enough energy to keep fighting. The others collapsed in the pale moonlight, beside a towering stack of reed baskets.

"For a wood frog, you've got spirit," Arabanoo said, puffing out his throat. "I'll give you that."

"And for a tree frog," Darel answered, "you're not afraid to get your toe pads dirty."

Arabanoo grinned and lunged forward.

Darel twirled and kicked at Arabanoo, catching him in the stomach. Arabanoo grunted, narrowed his nostrils, and tackled Darel. They tussled and rolled and smashed into the towering stack of reed baskets.

They heard a creaking. The snap of a corded vine.

They stopped fighting and looked at each other.

Then they looked at the stack of baskets toppling toward them.

After leaping to safety, they watched helplessly as the baskets avalanched downhill and crashed into the marketplace, overturning stalls of lily-pad furniture and smashing into carts full of candied worms, didgeridoos, and pollywog toys.

# 5

A PALE MOON SHONE OVER THE scorpion army's camp at the base of the spider queen's craggy mountain. A dozen warriors marched past tents made of tortoiseshell and frogskin, advancing toward Lord Marmoo's large pavilion.

The coarse sand shifted beneath the eight-legged warriors. They had razor-sharp pincers, but their deadliest weapons were the venom-tipped tails that swayed above them. And they didn't bother with shields—their leathery shells, called carapaces, were armor enough.

Torchlight glinted off the battered carapace of the scorpion in the lead—Commander Pigo, a massive warrior who, despite his size, moved with agility and deadly efficiency.

The soldiers scuttled behind him into the cavern-ous pavilion and stood at attention.

There was something particularly hard about the scorpion who lounged on the throne.

Lord Marmoo's carapace was crisscrossed with scars, and his main pair of eyes shone with bright malevolence while his three pairs of side eyes remained watchful. He'd seized control of the vast scorpion armies not only because he was the most merciless and venomous fighter but also because his mind was as sharp as his stinger.

Unlike the great majority of scorpions, he was patient. He planned, he plotted, he waited. And *then* he struck.

"Commander Pigo," he drawled in greeting. "The warriors are ready?"

"Always, my lord!" Pigo said.

"I know you find poetry boring, little brother, but have you ever heard the rhyme beginning 'Will you walk into my parlor?' said the spider to the fly?"

"I have not, my lord."

Lord Marmoo smiled lazily. "Shall I tell you what the fly said?"

"By all means, my lord."

"'Oh no, no,' said the little fly," Lord Marmoo continued, "'to ask me is in vain. For who goes up your winding stair can never come down again.'"

"No doubt a fine poem, my lord," said Pigo.

Lord Marmoo's gaze swept the soldiers. "And here we are, at the base of the spider's mountain. Do any of you fine warriors have a question for me?"

The warriors all remained silent, staring straight ahead.

"This won't do," Lord Marmoo said, tapping his pincers on the enormous crate beside the throne. "Surely at least *one* of you is brave enough to say a few words."

After another short silence, a sergeant said: "Permission to speak, sir!"

Pigo nodded slowly. "Granted."

The sergeant saluted him, then bowed to Lord Marmoo, lowering his forelegs to the ground. "My lord, I've served you faithfully since we were both scorplings."

"I remember those days well," Lord Marmoo said. "Eating our brothers and sisters until only the strong survived."

"And none stronger than you, my lord. But the spider queen is treacherous and uses cunning instead of strength."

"That she does, sergeant."

"She *invented* nightcasting, my lord. She was the

turtle king's favorite student before she betrayed him."

"Yes," Marmoo murmured, "and she turned his dreamcasting into a fiercer, darker magic."

The sergeant nodded. "They say she's almost as strong as him now."

"*Almost?* She'd kill you for suggesting that she's not already more powerful than the turtle king."

The sergeant's tail drooped. "Yes, my lord."

"So," Marmoo inquired, "are you afraid of walking into Queen Jarrah's parlor?"

"Um, no, my lord," the sergeant answered, his middle legs shifting beneath him. "For however strong she is, you're stronger. I simply . . . wanted to ask . . . about taking a guard of only a dozen scorpions into the spider's castle. Is it enough?"

Lord Marmoo nodded to Pigo. "Answer him, little brother."

Pigo lashed his tail through the air and stung the sergeant in the back of the neck. The sergeant dropped lifeless to the floor of the tent.

"Would anyone else like permission to speak?" Pigo asked. "To question his lordship?"

Absolute silence fell in the tent.

Lord Marmoo finally stood, with a swift, silky motion. "You see, my friends—'Walk into my parlor,' said the spider to the *fly*. We are not flies—we are scorpions. We join forces with Queen Jarrah because we are strong, not because we are weak. When I choose, we will bury the entire spider nation under the sands."

"Outside!" Commander Pigo barked at a signal from his leader. "Grab the crate, and prepare to climb!"

The soldiers hefted the enormous crate and filed past the sergeant's body. As they left, Pigo remained at attention next to Lord Marmoo's throne. But once they disappeared, he sighed, crossed to an ironwood table, and skewered a chunk of raw mouse from a platter.

"You're concerned, too?" Lord Marmoo asked, joining Pigo at the table.

"I am, my lord brother—that's my job." He lifted the meat toward his mandible-like mouthparts. "Should I sting myself for worrying about your safety?"

"Would you if I commanded it?"

"Without hesitation."

Lord Marmoo smiled. "I know you would, Pigo. You're the only one I trust. Of course the spiders are treacherous—I don't need a *sergeant* telling me that Queen Jarrah is dangerous."

"*Is* she as powerful as the turtle king?"

"According to her, yes," Marmoo said. "That's all

she cares about, defeating her former teacher. And King Sergu was old a hundred years ago, when he ruled this whole region. Even for a turtle, that's a long time, so he must be growing weaker."

"While Queen Jarrah is growing stronger . . ." Pigo skewered another chunk of mouse. "So this march across the desert to her mountain castle may be worth it, after all?"

"She says she's finally ready to defeat him. And she's not the only one getting stronger, is she?"

"No, my lord. Your army is ten times bigger than any scorpion horde since the time of legend."

"Indeed. But as our numbers increase, we drain the outback. We're running out of food and water. We need a more fertile land." Lord Marmoo's pincers snapped shut. "We need the Amphibilands, and soon it will be ours."

# 6

CHIEF OLBA LIVED IN THE CENTER of the village, in a modest leaf house with a spray of ferns in the front yard and a tidy pond in back. The inside of her house was mostly ordinary, with a few extra bedrooms for visitors, but one thing made it unique. Beyond the kitchen, an archway led into the village meeting hall, a lofty space with a roof of branches for the tree frogs, a leaf-lined cave mouth for the burrowers, and a spring for those frogs who grew nervous without water nearby. It was to the meeting hall that Olba summoned Darel after his mother bandaged his scrapes, her eyes heavy with disappointment.

Darel paused outside the hall, inflated his throat, and sighed. How come living by the warrior code wasn't *easier*?

All he wanted was to act like a Kulipari, strong and unafraid, but instead he had upset his mother and messed things up with his best friend. Oh, and destroyed the marketplace.

Still, nothing to do now but face the croaking.

A few frogs chatted quietly in the shadows of the great hall, and he didn't see Chief Olba at first. She was sitting on a flat stone bench in the talking circle. Then he spotted her: a shiny black frog with a red-crowned forehead that furrowed when she was concerned. It was furrowed now.

She patted the stone bench beside her, and Darel hopped across the hall and sat. After a long silence, the chief murmured, "You told me you wouldn't fight Arabanoo again."

"I guess I lost my temper, ma'am."

"They were picking on Gurnugan?"

"It's not Gee's fault! Don't blame him—he just does what I tell him."

"He *chooses* to do what you tell him."

"Ask Coorah," Darel said, shaking his head. "It's my fault, like always."

"Even Coorah is not always wise," Olba said. "She's still trying to learn battlefield medicine instead of pollywog care."

"Her grandmother told Coorah that she has a gift, and she needs to follow her heart," Darel explained. "And her heart tells her we're going to need the old

knowledge of war-healing. Her gran said the scorpions are coming back."

"Are you trying to change the subject?" the chief asked, her eyes bulging in amusement. "We're talking about you and Gurnugan."

"Oh, right." Darel inflated his throat. "Well, it's not Gee's fault. He just backed me up, because that's what friends do."

"Protecting a friend is nothing to be ashamed of. But tell me this, Darel. What if you must choose between doing the right thing and protecting a friend?"

"I guess I . . ." He flicked his inner eyelids. "I don't know."

The chief didn't say anything. She just sat there quietly.

Finally, he asked, "So what's the right answer? What should I do?"

"That is something we all must decide for ourselves." She tapped the stone bench with her finger pads. "Now, then . . . why didn't you give Arabanoo the honey snails?"

"Because I don't like bullies, and . . ."

"Yes?"

Darel shook his head. He didn't want to tell her why he was saving the snails. "Just because."

"Mmm. You realize that you're going to spend the next few months working to repay the peddlers in the marketplace for the damage you did?"

"Yes, ma'am." He added, hesitantly, "I can still practice in the evenings, though, right? If I don't get into fights?"

"Your father and I were like brother and sister," the chief said. "As close as you and Gurnugan. I think you know what he would tell you."

He sighed. "To help Mom in the shop."

Chief Olba didn't say anything. She didn't need to. They sat for a while in the cool quiet of the hall, listening to the soft croaking of conversations and the call of a distant night bird.

"Your father was a great frog, Darel," the chief said at last. "He's the reason we can sit safely in the moonlight and smell the night-blooming flowers. He and the other Kulipari gave their lives to help hide the Amphibilands behind the Veil."

"I just . . ." Darel swallowed. "I want to make him proud."

She smiled softly. "He would be."

"I'm not even a warrior."

"He fell in love with a *shopkeep*, Darel. And his best friend"—Olba patted her plump stomach—"never battled anything except her dinner. Do you know what he told me once?"

"What?"

"That wood frogs have their own powers."

"Like what?" Darel asked. "We can hide in the dirt?"

"You work harder than anyone," the chief told him. "You're brave and loyal, and you never give up. Look at you, Darel. Training every day to become a warrior."

Darel shrugged, pretending he didn't feel a warm glow of pride. "We've got to be ready if the scorps or spiders attack, that's all."

"Does part of you hope they will?"

"No! Of course not!" Darel scratched his cheek. "Well, maybe a little. I mean, just in my daydreams."

"Do you know what else your father told me? That he valued peace more than war."

"We *need* warriors, though. The next time the scorpions or spiders invade—"

"They can't find us."

"But—"

Olba raised a finger, silencing the young frog. "Even if they did—impossibly—find us, we'd beat them. As we have in the past."

"We *barely* beat them, though."

She smiled. "Don't underestimate the Kulipari."

"Where *are* the Kulipari? I know they went away and all—"

"They lost many warriors in the Hidingwar, Darel. Dozens of them died, like your father."

Darel looked at the floor.

"You remember how it happened," Chief Olba continued. "You were a young frog then. After the spider queen betrayed King Sergu, the scorpions launched a surprise attack. The Kulipari saved us, at great cost to themselves. They're rebuilding their numbers and regaining their strength."

"Okay, but, I mean—where?"

"With the turtle king. Why, there are probably a *hundred* of them by now! Imagine that, a hundred Kulipari."

Darel's throat bulged at the thought. A hundred Kulipari! Plus him: a hundred and *one*.

"And yet we don't need them." Chief Olba flicked an inner eyelid thoughtfully. "Not anymore. For more than a hundred years before the Hidingwar, the turtle king kept the peace between the scorpions and spiders, and he took extra care to protect the frog nation—we're tough, but we're fragile."

"Mostly tough," Darel said.

The chief inflated her throat in amusement. "We drink through our skin, Darel—we need pure water to survive. King Sergu helped us find a place to thrive here in the Amphibilands. Just like he taught the spiders dreamcasting because they understand webs of magic as well as they understand webs of silk."

"Except that didn't work so well."

The chief nodded. "It might have, but Jarrah turned the gentle magic of dreamcasting into the evil of nightcasting. She's a terrible creature now, filled with hunger and jealousy and power."

"Yeah, that's why we need the Kulipari."

"As long as the Veil stands, she cannot touch us," the chief said. "There's nothing to fear."

# 7

AREL WOKE EARLY AND SPENT the morning in the marketplace, getting scolded by each merchant as he cleaned the mess that had been made by the falling baskets. He swept and scrubbed, grumbling as other young frogs teased him. He stuck his tongue out at one and almost caught a passing mosquito.

Finally, at noon, he stopped and gobbled his lunch. Then he hopped over to the tadpool nursery to see the triplets.

The tadpool rippled in the shade of a paperbark tree—a dozen linked pools that echoed with shouts and laughter and occasionally tears.

Darel stopped and watched the pollywogs chasing one another in the shallows and the tadpoles waddling eagerly onto shore, where teachers were sitting in circles with students.

An older tadpole was showing off, hopping over some younger ones, when her tail got tangled in her

legs. She fell into the pond with a splash, emerging a moment later sputtering with embarrassment.

Darel smiled, reliving his first memories of his father, here at the nursery. Climbing all over the frog everyone else knew as the greatest Kulipari of his generation but Darel just knew as Daddy.

His memory was interrupted by calls of "Darel! Darel! Come play!"

The triplets swarmed toward him in shining blurs of color. Tharta, Tipi, and Thuma looked nothing like Darel—instead, they took after their father.

Tharta was bright pink with a row of spikes down her back, Tipi was mostly yellow with glossy green and orange swirls, and Thuma was a brilliant blue with black spots and stripes.

They hadn't even sprouted legs when Dad died, so Darel made a point of seeing them every day, playing games and passing down his father's war stories. They admired him with the blind adoration of little siblings and wanted to be just like him when they grew up.

They had no idea that *he* wanted to be just like *them*—poisonous.

In the old days, wood frogs like Darel didn't have poisonous brothers and sisters. Even before the turtle king raised the Veil, though, his dreamcasting had changed the Amphibilands. He'd united the frog tribes, and they'd begun to start families together.

Sometimes Darel thought that was as big a deal as the Veil—at least to him. Because without it, he and the triplets never could've had a wood frog mother and a poisonous father.

Thuma hugged him while Tharta and Tipi leaped into his arms, and he let them pull him into the water. He mock-scolded them for roughhousing, then chased them around the pool, playing Croako Polo until it was time to get back to work.

He spent the rest of the day hauling heavy bundles

of reeds for the furniture maker. He actually liked that job: good for building strength and endurance, and every time he set down another bundle, he threw a few punches at it.

Well, until the furniture maker caught him, that is. Then he got in trouble again.

Instead of returning home at the end of the day, Darel followed a weedy path across a stream. He turned toward the salt marsh at the northern tip of the Amphibilands, then stopped at a door beside a mossy stump.

He knocked and waited.

And waited.

And waited.

And eventually, the door opened.

Stale air wafted out at Darel. He smiled at the frog standing within, an elderly pond frog, now frail and fish-belly white, with clouded eyes and an unsteady gait. His name was Old Jir, and he'd been a Kulipari once, with bright green skin and copper spots, before the poison broke him.

"Is that you, Darel?" Old Jir wheezed, his pale eyes peering at him.

"Yes, sir," Darel said. "May I come inside? My feet are aching."

"Young liar," Old Jir scoffed fondly. "Your feet never ache. Where's your shadow?"

"Gee? He's ponded for approximately the rest of his life."

Old Jir chuckled and shuffled into the living room, a cramped space with a musty odor and dirty plates piled everywhere.

"I'm in trouble again," Darel said, opening the birch-bark curtains to air out the room.

"You, in trouble? Next you'll tell me that water's still wet."

Darel grinned and started stacking the dirty plates as the old frog lowered himself into a chair. He told Old Jir what had happened—leaving out nothing except the honey snails—and finished with "They're pretty mad at me."

"Good," the old frog croaked. "They need froglings like you to remind them that they're still alive."

"Really?"

"Of course—you hop around like a kangaroo with a spiny anteater in her pouch, Darel. You keep everyone on their toe pads. You're full of life." Old Jir raised his skeletal right hand and watched it tremble. "I remember how that feels."

Darel didn't want Old Jir to get into one of his moods, so he said, "Oh! I brought you some honey snails—your favorite." He emptied his pouch into a cleanish bowl. "Um, they're a little smooshed."

"You're a good boy, Darel."

"I'm glad *someone* thinks so." Darel took another load of bark dishes to the sink. "You know what everyone tells me? That we don't need warriors to fight the scorpions and spiders. Just hunters, for scaring off the snakes and birds."

Old Jir snatched at a honey snail with his tongue. "There were birds during the Hidingwar, waiting to swoop down on the wounded. And the turtle king was there, riding on his crocodile, surrounded by scorpions. A thousand of them, tails stinging, pincers slashing. The king closed his eyes in the middle of the battle—do you know why?"

"He was dreamcasting."

"Of course he was dreamcasting!" the old frog snapped. "He's a dreamcaster. But what was he using his magic *for*?"

"To hide the Amphibilands. To raise the Veil like a . . . a shell around us, to keep the scorpions and spiders out."

"The Veil isn't a shell, frogling; it's not an invisible wall you can bounce stones off. It's a trick of the mind that confuses the enemy when he gets too close. The scorps and spiders look, but they don't see us. They march in a straight line and end up right back where they started. The Veil is a blind spot, that's all."

"And in the old days . . . ," Darel prompted, knowing how much Old Jir liked telling his stories.

"Before the Veil, when you were just a tadpole, the scorps and spiders knew where to find us. We fought skirmishes, but the turtle king always stepped in before things went too far. Back then, the scorpions didn't want to kill us all and take our land."

"Not until the Hidingwar," Darel said.

"Do you know what caused the Hidingwar?" asked Old Jir.

Darel shook his head.

"The scorps started running out of food and water," Old Jir told him. "They wanted our waterfalls and woodlands, our ponds and farms. In those days, they sent merchants to trade. I remember one of them staring at the nursery pools. She couldn't believe we 'wasted' fresh water on tadpoles."

"So what did they do?"

"They waited until the spider queen made her move. Jarrah thought she could kill the turtle king, but he's a tough old shellback. He beat her. She still hates him for that, still wants her revenge." Old Jir turned his clouded gaze toward Darel. "What weapons do the scorpions and the spiders have, what powers?"

"Well, the scorpions have shells as strong as ironwood. They have poison stingers and powerful pincers." Darel thought for a second. "Don't they have a bunch of extra eyes?"

"They have a pair of main eyes and between two and five pairs of side eyes. What about the spiders?"

"They're great with webs, obviously. And they're

poisonous, too—at least some of them. Plus the night-casting."

Old Jir scratched a wart on his forehead. "And what do we have?"

"The Kulipari?"

"What do *ordinary* frogs have, Darel?"

"Um, we croak?"

The old frog slitted his nostrils. "What else?"

"We jump? And our tongues are pretty fast."

"Even faster than a scorpion's stinger," Old Jir said, with a nod. "We're clever and hardworking, and we come in all shapes and sizes. Tree frogs and burrowers, bullfrogs and corroborees."

"What does that matter?"

"It makes us flexible. We have many different strengths." Old Jir inflated his throat. "And we think for ourselves. The scorpions aren't like that."

"You mean they're stupid?"

"No, they're often cunning, but they follow a leader blindly. If the leader falls, they retreat. If nobody gives them orders, they don't know what to do."

"Like I said—stupid."

Old Jir croaked a soft laugh. "Plus, we know this land, Darel, we know every tree and stream. And you forgot a few things that the spiders and scorps have."

"Like what? Armies and weapons?"

"No—endless sand and lifeless rock. A long time ago, the desert was grassland and trees, rich soil and deep rivers, but they used everything up. They turned their home into a wasteland."

"And now they want *our* home," Darel said.

"That's right—that's why they attacked. The scorpion army swept down from the outback, more of them than we imagined possible. And the Hidingwar began. Hungry birds flew overhead, and the turtle king's crocodile snapped her jaws and lashed her tail."

"What'd the king do?" Darel asked, his eyes bulging.

"He sat on her back, his face calm, his eyes closed, dreamcasting in the middle of a pitched battle, creating the Veil. The scorpions killed his croc in the end, and they were about to finish off the king, when we showed up. The Kulipari."

Darel gave a little excited hop. This was his favorite part of the story.

"I was old even then," Old Jir continued, "but strong. We tapped the poison and dropped on them like an avalanche. Your father stood alone against a whole battalion and crushed them. But the scorpion army had been growing in the black hills, bigger than any army we'd ever faced before. And you know the limits of our poison, don't you?"

"If you use it too much . . ." Darel couldn't finish.

"We die. Or we live, drained of all power. Broken shells of who we were—like me."

"But you beat the scorpions."

Old Jir sighed. "That we did. Most of the Kulipari died, including your father, and yet—"

"Are you sure?" Darel blurted, inflating his throat in surprise that he'd finally asked the question aloud.

"About what?"

"That—that my dad died?" He took a breath and continued. He couldn't look at the old frog. He was afraid to see his expression. "They never found the body. I mean, after the battle. And I've always wondered if maybe he lived, like you. Just without his powers?"

Old Jir reached out and squeezed Darel's arm. "I'm sorry, Darel. No, your father gave his life to help win the final battle."

Darel kept his eyes on the floor, blinking back tears. His hope that his father was still out there somewhere was a secret wish he'd held close for a long time. It hurt to hear the truth.

"At least we saved the turtle king's life," Old Jir

said, gently. "And his dreamcasting took root—he raised the Veil. Your father's sacrifice saved us all."

Darel gulped and wiped his eyes.

"We won't see the scorps again." Old Jir sat back. "Instead of fighting, all we've got are the dried-up stories of dried-up frogs."

"I *like* your stories."

But Old Jir was in a mood now, and his mouth tightened into an unhappy line. Maybe thinking about his own lost powers. Maybe thinking about Darel's dad.

"They're right, you know," the old frog said, closing his inner eyelids. "Training for battle is a waste of time. And that's a good thing, Darel. Now you run along and leave an old frog in peace."

# 8

THE SCORPIONS ADVANCED THROUGH the mountain pass. Commander Pigo scuttled one step behind Lord Marmoo, while the warriors carrying the enormous crate brought up the rear. Shaggy-barked blackwood trees crowded the path, and a butcher-bird cried in the distance, near the sandstone cliffs.

The moon rose higher as they climbed through a stinking swamp swirling with black water too bitter to drink. When spiders skittered among the shadows, the scorpion warriors coiled their tails, eager to fight their ancient enemy, and only Lord Marmoo's presence stopped them from attacking.

After the swamp, they passed the dark mouths of Queen Jarrah's mines and the filthy huts of the miners forced to work underground, digging for gems. The spider guards shifted uneasily, coiling strands of silk from their abdomens, and Pigo watched them with his side eyes, wary of an ambush.

But the spiders didn't attack. Perhaps the cease-fire would hold and the scorpions would be able to work with the spiders . . . for a time, at least.

From a distance, the mountaintop looked to Pigo like a sprawling heap of rocks, but as they marched closer, he saw that each rock was a boulder, as high and wide as Lord Marmoo's pavilion. This was the spiders' castle: thousands of boulders massed together. The spider queen and her court lived in the spaces between them, the cracks and crevices, corridors and caverns.

A wide moat of spiderweb surrounded the boulder castle, shimmering on the ground.

Pigo called his soldiers to a halt, and worker spiders placed a walkway of planks on the web for them to cross. Once inside the castle, they'd be trapped—but a scorpion warrior does not show fear, so Pigo ordered his troops forward without hesitation.

Cool air wafted from the shadowy entrances to the castle, smelling of incense and blood. The scorpions entered a vaulted hall, where Queen Jarrah greeted them with haughty politeness.

"Welcome to my home, Lord Marmoo," she said, creeping closer. "You *are* a brawny one, aren't you? Quite formidable, I'm sure."

"The better to join our forces," he replied.

"Oh, most certainly," Jarrah agreed. "That's how we'll both achieve our goals. By adding the brute strength of your scorpion hordes to the unstoppable magic of my nightcasting."

She was tall and slender and striking, with sharp features and arching eyebrows. And when she invited Pigo and Lord Marmoo to watch her nightcasting, her voice sounded like one of her webs: silky and deceptively strong.

Three of her ladies-in-waiting—her most loyal servants and most skilled apprentice nightcasters—accompanied them as they climbed higher within the castle. The ladies occasionally strolled along the walls or the ceiling, until they all stepped onto a platform atop the highest boulder of the castle, with a view of the surrounding countryside.

"Lord Marmoo." Queen Jarrah had crept up beside him. "I hope you approve of the view?"

Marmoo bent his forelegs slightly and peered into the distance. "Breathtaking. Wouldn't you agree, commander?"

"Useful for spotting enemies," Pigo said, rubbing his chin with his pincers. "As they approach."

"You don't find it beautiful?" Queen Jarrah asked, a little sharply.

"Very much so, my lady." But Pigo didn't care about beauty; he only cared about the upcoming invasion. "And from here, your nightcasting will tear down the Veil protecting the Amphibilands?"

"If she is successful," Lord Marmoo said.

"I will succeed," she told him, "if you have brought me what I need. And if you guarantee my payment."

"We're allies now, Queen Jarrah. United with a single purpose."

"United with a *double* purpose," she corrected. "For you wish to conquer the Amphibilands, but I have a different goal."

"You want the turtle king dead."

"The *dreamcaster*." She spat the word like a curse. "He thinks he's more powerful than I am? He beat me once, but I'll show him what power is. He uses *visions* to change the world. I use webs and poison. He'll soon discover which is stronger."

"Once you destroy the Veil, Queen Jarrah, my army will slaughter the frogs in their wetland home. And even though the turtle king is old and weak, there's no doubt that he'll come forward to protect them."

"Yes," she said, with a sharp nod. "He's coddled those pathetic frogs for a hundred years. That's the only reason they've survived."

"Well, soon King Sergu will leave his Turtle Coves to try to save them. And you will ensnare him."

"*If*," Queen Jarrah repeated, "you have brought me what I need."

She prowled toward a small boulder standing beside the enormous crate the scorpions warriors had brought. She drew a single strand of silk from her abdomen, smeared it with poison, then draped it across the boulder.

The flimsy thread fell gently across the rough rock and—

*Crack!* The boulder split apart with a loud report.

The noise faded, and Pigo gaped. The boulder looked as if a giant blade had cleaved it cleanly in two: Both halves were facing skyward, the cut surfaces perfectly smooth.

A moment later, spider warriors scaled the castle walls, climbing onto the platform. They lifted the crate and poured the contents—dirt and rock—onto the two halves of the divided boulder.

"Imprints of everything that ever happened still mark the earth," Queen Jarrah said. "Imprints of a mouse running from an owl. Imprints of a crocodile killing a kangaroo. Even imprints of a dreamcasting remain in the dirt and soil. And those imprints teach lessons."

"Do you understand, Pigo?" Lord Marmoo asked, his segmented tail cocked inquisitively.

Pigo nodded slowly. "She's going to use this dirt to study the imprints of the turtle king's dreamcasting? To learn how he did it?"

"Very good," the queen said. "You're smarter than you look. The turtle king protected the Amphibilands well, but if I can catch the imprints of his casting in my web, then I can undo it."

"She needed the soil from the place where he stood

while casting his magic," Lord Marmoo explained. "From that very spot on the battlefield. And finally . . ." He gestured to the dirt-heaped boulder with one battered claw. "I found it."

The spider queen raised her thin arms, and a hush fell. "Oh, yes," she whispered. "This will do nicely."

As she tapped her poison for nightcasting power, shiny dark spots bloomed in her eyes until they were completely black. She started circling the boulder halves, drawing strand after strand of silk from her spinnerets.

She stroked the dirt, shuttling around and around until a web took form. Then she smiled, and her fangs extended, glistening with poison.

A droplet fell onto the web, and the silk shimmered and swirled.

Pigo saw shapes form on the churning web, toxic patterns that spread, twisted, and withered. And finally, the nightcasting was over.

The queen's eyes returned to normal. Weak from the effort, she collapsed onto a webbed stool her ladies-in-waiting had spun. She sank her fangs into a wriggling silken bundle—some unfortunate wasp caught earlier—and drank her fill.

Then she raised her venomous gaze to Lord

Marmoo and smiled icily. "The turtle king will soon writhe in my web."

"You learned how to destroy his dreamcasting?"

"I learned how to weaken it. The Veil has many layers, Lord Marmoo. I can tear down the outermost ones now, but I need one more thing before I destroy it completely. I need something from *inside* the Amphibilands, something alive and rooted to the froglands: a waratah tree in bloom."

"But that's impossible." Marmoo's mouthparts clicked in frustration. "I've marched a thousand regiments toward the Amphibilands, but we can't enter."

"Starting tomorrow, you can. Just the edges, at first, where I've frayed the Veil."

Lord Marmoo's tail quivered in anticipation. "Then you shall have your tree. And after you do, my queen, how long until you destroy the turtle king's magic completely?"

"Not long at all, after I'm in position at the Veil," she told him. "I must get close if I am to tear it down."

Lord Marmoo turned to Pigo. "Gather my armies. Hire every mercenary, from the desert to the sea. We meet at the site of the last battle."

"And then, my lord?"

"And then, little brother—we march."

## 9

GEE'S RAMBLING, LEAFY HOME stood at the top of a lawn that sloped to the bank of the river. He lived with his parents and grandparents, seven brothers and sisters, and assorted cousins, aunts, and uncles. His family were builders, so whenever a relative needed space, they just built a new addition.

Which was nice, because it gave Darel plenty of hiding spots to use if he wanted to approach unnoticed. As he did now.

He crept through the bushes, then crossed a bark-lined path behind the most recently added wing of the house. The raspy calls of pink-and-white cockatoos rummaging for seeds on the lawn filled the air, and a shout sounded from the riverbank.

Darel froze, afraid he'd been spotted. Then he exhaled in relief—the shout had come from a couple of Gee's cousins splashing in the shallows. A moment later he crouched low, spread his toes, and sprang upward.

He flashed through the air and landed on top of the house, clinging tightly to the overlapping leaf shingles. He tiptoed across three sloping roofs to the main house, then dangled headfirst off the side, his toe pads gripping the reed gutter above him.

Leaning closer to a window, he softly croaked, "Wake up, you web-toed wombat."

"Darel!" Gee said, from inside. "What are you *doing*?"

Darel swung into Gee's bedroom, a messy nook with firefly lamps and a lily-pad bed.

"Visiting you," Darel said, flopping onto the bed.

"You know I'm ponded," Gee said. "If my dad hears you, he'll shout the warts off me."

"Nah," Darel told him. "He'll shout the warts off *me*. Like that time he caught us sneaking into the beetle barn."

Gee grinned. "You jumped a mile when he slammed those barn doors open."

"Yeah," Darel said, lying back on the bed. "I don't know why he always blames me."

"Because everything's always your fault?"

Darel chuckled. "That explains it."

Then he closed his eyes and let himself relax. Sometimes he thought that Gee's room was the only place he ever really felt peaceful. Just lazing around, chatting about nothing. Even listening to the distant croaking of Gee's extended family calmed him—the bickering and yelling and aimless rib-beting.

He smiled to himself and said, "I need to get Coorah those wattleflowers."

"What does she want with them?"

"They're for a medicine she's making. She found the recipe in her grandmother's stuff. You know how she gets."

"Yeah, she gets crazy ideas," Gee said. "Like you."

Darel threw a pillow at Gee, but what he said was kind of true. Coorah's grandmother had treated injured frogs on the battlefield, and she'd begged her granddaughter not to let the knowledge die out. Coorah had taken the request to heart, often neglecting the other healing arts her father hoped to teach her, like treating bellyaches and sprained tongues and scraped warts. He thought there wasn't any use for battlefield medicine anymore and that Coorah should stick to everyday ailments. But she kept studying her grandmother's books.

"Not crazy," Darel told Gee. "Determined."

"Goofier than a duck-billed platypus."

*"Anyway,"* Darel said, "I need wattleflowers. Have you seen any?"

"The only flowers I like," Gee informed him, "are the edible kind."

"Maybe I'll try over by the billabong." A billabong was a little lake that had split off from a river. "Or the beach."

"You just want an excuse to go hopping around all over creation."

"You know it." Darel grinned. "So are you coming?"

"I can't! I'm ponded."

"Sneak out."

Gee sighed. "My parents are making me work in the shop."

"Putting together twig tents again?"

"Yeah," Gee said, frowning. "I wish they'd let me work on the bungalows."

Darel nodded but didn't say anything. Part of him wanted to push Gee to join him, but sometimes he thought the only reason Gee was still making twig tents instead of cooler buildings was because he spent so much time sparring with Darel.

On the other hand, Gee hated making twig tents. So encouraging him to sneak off would be doing him a favor.

Still, Darel didn't mention wattleflowers again. The truth was, Gee had gotten ponded because of Darel. If he wanted to do his friend a favor, Darel would have to think of a way not to get him into more trouble. Something cooler than hopping around the billabong or the beach.

# 10

AREL KNEW HOW TO SNEAK INTO Gee's house but not his own. The bell over the front door jingled as he stepped inside. The front room of the house doubled as his mother's small, tidy shop.

"How'd things go at the market today?" his mother asked from her seat in the corner.

She greeted customers from her sitting nook and offered them twig tea and conversation as she took their orders. Her shop sold "flies for all occasions"— snack platters and wedding bouquets and children's games.

"Pretty good," Darel said. "I'm getting the hang of making furniture from bulrushes, and I like decorating the water toys. Making all those wart creams is tough, though."

"I thought you were sweeping and carrying."

Darel sat beside her. "Well, I got curious and started asking questions . . ."

His mother croaked a soft laugh. "You've always been as curious as an emu. A few of the crafters are wondering if you're interested in an apprenticeship."

Darel saw that his mother was making flysicles for a kid's birthday party. He began to help. "Really? That's kind of cool."

"Are you interested?"

"Nah. If I was going to apprentice to anyone, I'd apprentice to you." He jabbed his thumb pad on a stick. "Ow."

"I'm not sure I'd hire you," his mother teased.

"Yeah." He grinned. "Maybe I should stick to party platters."

They worked quietly for a time, exchanging the occasional word but mostly just enjoying each other's company. His mom moved to work on a pin-gñat-a, a leaf-box filled with gnats that kids broke open for the snacks inside. Darel finished the flysicles and started making a butterfly bouquet. He sometimes forgot how his mother seemed to slow everything down. As if, no matter how busy things got, there was plenty of time and no need to run around like an emu in a thunderstorm.

Except the thought reminded Darel that he actually *did* need to run around. "Oh!" he said.

"Jab yourself again?"

"No, I just remembered something I need to do."

She finished the pin-gñat-a. "Do I want to know?"

"It's nothing *bad*. I just need to get Coorah a wattleflower."

"Oh, really? Well, she is a very pretty young frog."

"Mom! Not like *that*! I owe her a flower, that's all."

"Charming, too. And she's already quite a skilled healer, like her father—even if she is as busy preparing for an imaginary war as you are." His mother shooed him away. "Now run along and collect that flower, if you must."

Darel looked at the stack of work. "You don't mind?"

"I'm perfectly capable of managing the shop alone."

"Well, the thing is . . . I looked in all the regular spots today and couldn't find the kind she wants—the yellow ones with the red tips. She needs them for a medicine she's working on."

His mother's inner eyelids flicked. "You're talking about going to the Outback Hills?"

"Well, yeah," he admitted. "But just the first hill. That's completely inside the Amphibilands. It's totally safe."

"The Veil runs through the third hill, Darel."

"Yeah, two hills over. I'm just going to pick some flowers." He thought for a second. "Well, plus Gee is ponded because of me, so I'm going to try to take him along."

His mother flicked her eyelids again. "I thought you were doing this for Coorah."

"Well, I'm catching two flies with one lick," Darel said.

"Have his parents agreed?" she asked, dubiously.

"Not yet."

"You take care of Gee, Darel," she said. "You know he looks up to you."

He nodded. "I will."

"All the way to the Hills, huh?"

"I know I messed up with the white-lipped frogs," he told her. "But I'm not going to mess with the Veil. I promise."

"Come here." She set aside her work and kissed him on the forehead. "I trust you. I always have."

"So I can go?"

"Well, it *is* the weekend. You can go tomorrow morning. I'll pack you lunch."

# 11

ARLY THE NEXT MORNING, DAREL hopped across town and knocked on Gee's front door.

He was eager to start the trip—and he wanted to catch Gee's mom at home. She always said that he was a bad influence, but she said it as if it was a *good* thing.

Gee's dad, on the other hand, just didn't like him. So of course he was the one who opened the door.

He took one look at Darel, then narrowed his nostrils and said, "No."

Darel gulped. "Good morning, sir—"

"No."

"Um, I'm just wondering—"

"No."

From inside the house, Gee's mom called, "Is that Darel? Are you going to stand there like a koala in a cactus, or are you going to invite him in?"

"Going to stand here," Gee's dad said.

Gee's mom appeared in the doorway and said, "You know he's ponded, Darel."

"Yes, ma'am," he said. "Only I'm hopping to the eucalyptus forest today, and, um, it's pretty good exercise."

Which he said because he knew Gee's parents worried about his weight. But when he told them he was hiking *through* the eucalyptus forest to the Outback Hills, Gee's father grumbled.

"If you take one step too far," he said, "every scorpion and spider in a hundred miles will see you."

"I know, sir. I won't go too far."

"You always go too far. You act like a sandpaper frog half the time."

Darel wanted to croak a denial, but before he could say anything, Gee's mom spoke.

"That's not fair," she said, a little sharply. "You name one time he got Gurnugan in *real* trouble."

"The day will come," Gee's father said. "Mark my words."

"We'll be extra careful," Darel assured him. "Just the first hill and no farther."

"I don't know . . . ," Gee's mother said. "He's still ponded."

"How about this?" Darel asked, taking a breath. "You let Gee come along, and once I'm done at the marketplace, I'll work for you for a week."

"Hmm," Gee's mother said, eyeing him with interest. "That's not a bad idea."

"Oh, no . . . ," Gee's father muttered.

"Bringing Darel to work will be the best way to get Gurnugun excited about the family business," Gee's mom told her husband, "and you know it."

"True enough," Gee's father croaked.

Gee's mother touched Darel's arm. "Work for us for a *month*," she said, "and it's a deal."

Darel hesitated. He didn't want to waste a month working for the construction company. But he thought of all the times Gee sparred with him even though he didn't really enjoy it.

So he said, "Can we work on bungalows and cottages instead of twig tents?"

Gee's mom bulged her throat. "After the first week."

"Then you've got a deal," Darel said, with a sudden grin.

Three seconds later, Gee bounded down the curving staircase, a bulging pack slung over one shoulder. "Thanks, Mom! Thanks, Dad! See you tonight!"

Gee bustled through the front door, dragging Darel toward the street. "Quick, before they make us take Miro."

"Were you listening the whole time?"

"And packing. I brought sweets!"

"Cool."

"Well, you got me out of a day of being ponded. Plus, we get to work on *bungalows*!"

Darel chuckled.

Gee chattered excitedly as they hopped past the marketplace. A few of the vendors called greetings as they left the village.

They jumped toward the cool air flowing from the waterfall above the village, and Darel told Gee just how terrible he'd been at making reed chairs, the first six tries. "The seventh time, though," he said, while they crossed the river, "the chair I made was so good, she's going to sell it."

"That's pretty cool."

"Yeah, except she's selling it as a jungle gym for froglets."

They stopped for an early lunch beyond the water-fall, in a glade of horsetail ferns. From there, the trail rose toward the hills, and the sharp scent of eucalyptus wafted around them. They set off again, and soon they

were in the eucalyptus forest itself. The graceful trees towered overhead, trunks shedding bark and slender leaves flitting through the sunlight to the ground.

"I hope we see a yellow-bellied glider," Gee said.

Gliders were nocturnal opossums that lived only in the eucalyptus forests. They had long tails, pointy ears, and flaps of skin that let them swoop through the air from one tree to another.

"They sleep during the day," Darel reminded him.

"Oh, right." Gee sighed. "Maybe if we walk really slow, we'll see them on the way back. Ooh, or the little red bats!"

Darel didn't have the heart to remind Gee that of course the bats, too, were nocturnal. "I heard they're nomadic," he said, a little wistfully. "They travel wherever they want, even outside the Veil."

Gee gazed into the shadowed woods nervously, his eyes bulging more than usual. "Just as long as nothing from out there gets in here."

"The Veil will protect us. We're nowhere near the border, Gee."

"I guess."

"The eucalyptus forest is huge," Darel said, gesturing. "As big as the rest of the Amphibilands put together, even if the only villages are the tree frogs' by the creeks and the Baw Baws' in the bog."

"How do you know all this?"

"A warrior's gotta learn the lay of the land."

"You're weird."

"But I'm quick!" Darel said, and leaped ahead.

"Hey," Gee cried, racing after him.

# 12

DAREL AND GEE HOPPED UPHILL along the forest path until they finally stopped for a rest in the shade of a cherry shrub that was growing from the roots of a eucalyptus.

As they polished off a snack, a hunting party of barred frogs crept through the leaf litter, carrying the body of a brown snake.

Darel and Gee eyed the dead snake. "Where'd you catch him?" Gee asked.

"West of here," the lead hunter said. "These are the second-baddest snakes in Australia, boys. The only snakes more venomous are the taipans, and they keep to themselves."

"We don't usually see brown snakes inside the Veil," another hunter said, his warty brow furrowed in concern.

"Is the forest safe now?" Gee asked, biting his lip.

"For a couple of strong young frogs like you?" The

lead hunter winked an inner eyelid. "Stay near the path and you'll be fine."

The hunters waved good-bye, and the two friends lazed around, comparing strategies about how *they* would handle a brown snake. In the end they decided that one more snack was called for. Then, at last, they set off again.

Darel daydreamed as they hopped along: his favorite daydream of standing in the desolate outback, single-handedly facing a scorpion army that swept forward like the tide, then pulling a sword and cutting them down by the dozen—leaping and slashing and stabbing like the deadliest Kulipari. As always, the daydream ended with Darel in the ornate court of the turtle king, receiving a massive medal for his victory.

The path grew steeper as they approached the Outback Hills, three wooded peaks that rose sharply over the forest.

The first hill, where the wattleflowers grew, fell completely within the Amphibilands.

The second hill also fell completely within the Amphibilands—though Darel's mom never allowed him to explore that far.

The third hill, however, fell only halfway within the Amphibilands. On the far side of the third Outback

Hill, the desert scrub started—and the dreamcast Veil ended.

Darel didn't understand how the turtle king hid them. He didn't understand how the scorpions could wander to the border of the Amphibilands and not find it. But he understood that if any frog stepped across that edge, he put himself in deadly peril. So he made sure he knew exactly where he and Gee were.

The wattleflower Coorah wanted grew on the first ridge.

When they reached the top, Gee gulped. "Wow."

Darel followed his gaze.

The green meadows and valleys and forests of the Amphibilands were behind them. Ahead was the vast Australian outback, all tans and yellows and golds as far as the eye could see. It looked like it could swallow a frog and not notice.

Gee shivered. "Scary."

"Yeah," Darel said, though he didn't really agree. When he looked at the desert, he saw a stark beauty. "That's where they fought the final battle of the Hidingwar. Down there somewhere."

"What's that?" Gee asked, pointing at a distant shimmering over the dunes.

"A mirage, I guess," Darel said. "Oh! There's the wattleflower!"

They climbed the ridge toward a shrub bristling with brush-like flowers, bright yellow with red tips.

Darel cut six blooms for Coorah.

"I thought you only owed her one," Gee said.

"Yeah, but she's working on—*No!*" Darel suddenly croaked, staring into the distance with bulging eyes. "It can't be."

"What?" Gee shaded his eyes with his hand. "The mirage?"

"That's no mirage," Darel said, his voice barely louder than a whisper. "Those are scorpions . . . thousands of scorpions."

Gee looked closer and fearfully inflated his throat. "Th-th-they can't see us. You know they c-c-can't see us."

"Look at them. They're like the ocean. They could wipe us out in a day."

"But they can't f-f-find us. They don't know where we are."

"Then why are they heading this way?"

"It's a coincidence," Gee said. "It's a—a—" He fell silent, an expression of horror on his face. He raised one arm and pointed a trembling finger pad. Not into the distance but at the next hilltop, an arrow's flight away.

Four scorpion warriors were swarming over the peak: *inside* the Veil.

Three big scarred warriors scanned the countryside, venomous tails cocked and battle nets coiled in readiness. The fourth scorpion, even tougher-looking and clearly in charge, chopped the air with his pincers as he issued orders.

Darel's throat tightened, and his hands clenched.

*Scorpions*, inside the Amphibilands! Every instinct told him to leap away, but he breathed the way Old Jir had taught him. In and out, through his fear-clamped throat, until he could think again.

Gee jerked when Darel touched his arm.

"Go," Darel whispered. "Leap, Gee, as fast as you can. Tell the chief."

Gee gulped a few times, then bounded toward the eucalyptus forest. He stopped when he realized that Darel wasn't following.

"C'mon," he whispered. "Hurry!"

"I'm not going."

"W-w-what are you doing?"

"I'm going closer," Darel said, his heart pounding in his chest. "To hear what they're planning."

# 13

ITH THE STEALTH OF A warrior, Darel hopped through the woodland, tracking the enemy ahead. But this was no game. This was four terrifying scorpions, armed with claws and stingers.

Moving smoothly despite the terrified beating of his pulse, Darel dropped down the ravine between the first and second hills, gripping branches with his toe pads, skulking through the underbrush. He got into position and vaulted across the gulch, using the skills he'd learned from climbing the banyan tree.

Then he gathered his courage and crept toward the scorpions at the peak of the second hill.

They were still gathered on an outcropping, and at first Darel didn't understand the sounds he heard, a sort of gravelly chopping, a rhythmic *chuk, chuk, chuk.*

Darel touched his dagger for reassurance, dropped to his belly, and crawled forward in the fallen leaves.

When he peeked through a shrub, he saw a flash of movement.

The scorpions, not twenty feet away.

They were *digging*. Two of the warriors were digging around the base of a waratah tree with long green leaves and bright red flowers.

The commander was barking orders at them as he paced, his legs clacking over the ground.

"Go deeper—she needs the roots, too." The commander paced toward the shrub where Darel was hidden. "Dig under the tree, and we'll tear up the whole thing."

He was just a few feet from Darel.

Darel stopped breathing. His heart clenched. Through fear-widened eyes he saw the commander's carapace-armored legs.

And at that moment, more than anything, he wanted to be home.

He wanted to be splashing in the nursery with the triplets or cleaning trash in the marketplace or even tussling with Arabanoo. He wanted to be sitting with his mother in the cool, quiet shop, setting up games like moth-toss and tongue-of-war.

*No.* He inhaled slowly. *Get hold of yourself.*

*Act like a Kulipari.*

The eight gleaming legs shifted on the other side of the shrub, and Darel imagined the scorpion's many-eyed gaze scanning the woodland, then falling on him. He imagined the poison stinger blurring forward to strike.

Instead, the commander clattered away. Darel almost wept in relief, thrilled for once to be a wood frog, blending invisibly with the forest floor.

After a long, slow exhalation, he realized the scorpion commander was speaking again, explaining to one of his soldiers: ". . . because this isn't an ordinary waratah tree."

The soldier looked at the tree. "If you say so, Commander Pigo."

"Well, the tree is ordinary," the commander growled, "but *she* is not."

"She, sir?"

"Queen Jarrah."

The soldier snapped his pincers in disgust. "The spider queen."

"Don't worry," the one called Pigo said. "Lord Marmoo will kill her the moment she's no longer needed. But right now, she's useful. She can read imprints in the tree."

"Huh?"

"Her nightcasting frayed the outer layers of the Veil here," Pigo said, "but we can't go farther into the froglands until we bring her this tree. Because you know what happened to *this* tree, soldier?"

"No, sir."

"The turtle king's spell seeped into it. After she gets *this* in her web"—with a foreleg, he kicked an exposed root of the tree—"she'll tear down the Veil completely."

"The turtle's not going to stop her?"

"He's old and frail. By the time he realizes what's happening, the Amphibilands will be ours."

A coil of panic tightened in Darel's stomach. The spider queen knew how to rip the Veil apart! After she tore it down, the scorpion army would rampage through the Amphibilands, destroying every village and shop and home, leaving no frog alive.

He backed away through the underbrush, his mind blank with terror, and—

A crashing sounded nearby, and with a new spike of fear Darel realized that he'd made a stupid and potentially deadly mistake. He'd seen the commander and three scorpion warriors from the first Outback

Hill, but now there were only the commander and two warriors on the outcropping.

So where was the fourth? Patrolling through the underbrush directly toward *him*, that's where.

Darel dove into a pile of leaves and went absolutely still.

The crashing grew louder until the scorpion skittered into view, holding his battle net against his armored body.

"Soldier!" Commander Pigo barked from above. "You call that stealth? Every enemy within a mile will hear you."

"I already met the enemy, sir," the soldier said.

"Frogs?"

"Yes, sir." The soldier stepped onto the outcropping. "A hunting party, coming this way. They caught one glimpse of me and fled like cowards. I chased them, trying to sting the leader, but—"

"That wouldn't have stopped them," Pigo interrupted. "Killing a leader doesn't stop frogs."

"What?" The soldier looked baffled. "You can't keep fighting if your commander is down."

Pigo snapped one of his claws in disgust. "Frogs do. They have no honor, no respect for commanders and kings."

"Disgusting," the soldier said. "But I couldn't catch the leader, in any case. I kept getting turned around."

"You were running into the Veil," Pigo said.

"There's good news too, sir." The scorpion soldier tossed his net to the ground. "I grabbed *this*."

Inside the webbing wriggled Gee.

"Ah, a nice chunky frogling," Commander Pigo said, his mouthparts clattering. "Just in time for dinner."

# 14

PEEKING FROM UNDER THE PILE of leaves, Darel felt his nostrils close and his throat tighten. They'd captured Gee, and they were going to eat him.

Darel watched Gee's eyes bulge with terror, and he saw the scorpion warrior smack Gee until he stopped struggling. Darel wanted to blink and discover that none of this was really happening. He wanted that more than he'd ever wanted anything in his life: a do-over, a second chance.

Except after he blinked—first with his inner eyelids, then with his outer ones—nothing had changed.

*Okay.* Darel exhaled slowly. Despite all the training and practice and daydreams, despite knowing a scorp's only weakness was its underbelly, he wasn't ready.

He couldn't fight off one battle-scarred scorpion, much less four. He'd have to use stealth. He'd creep through the underbrush and cross the outcropping without being seen. Then he'd cut the net with his dagger and drag Gee away.

As the scorp warriors dug and the commander paced, Darel told himself to start moving. His legs refused to budge, though, and his hands refused to stop trembling.

He closed his eyes and exhaled, trying to calm himself. A Kulipari never left a fellow warrior behind, and Darel wasn't about to abandon his best friend.

He crept slowly around roots and hillocks, his belly on the ground, going absolutely motionless when one of the warriors raised a shiny black head. The foreign scent of desert wind blew over the Outback Hills from the dunes, and Darel imagined he could hear the shuffle of thousands of scorpion feet.

Soon that wouldn't be only in his imagination. Soon they'd come.

And with that thought, Darel realized what he and the other frogs needed to do: Warn the turtle king.

The turtles lived in the Coves, not far north of the Amphibilands, protected from the scorpion hordes by a mangrove swamp and protected from the spider armies by the turtle king: Sergu, greatest of the dream-casters. And the fact that the turtles rode crocodiles into battle probably didn't hurt.

In the old days, the turtles and the frogs had worked and traded and played together. But since the Hidingwar, no turtle except Sergu could find the Amphibilands, and no frog except the Kulipari would dare leave it.

Except now some frogs *must* dare.

Now Darel needed to convince the chief to send messengers racing across dangerous territory, to beg old King Sergu for help.

But first he needed to save Gee.

Twenty minutes later, he was crouching in a spiny-branched shrub, his skin blending with the sunburned leaves.

Fifteen feet away from him, in the shadow of the now-fallen waratah tree, Gee lay on his side inside the battle net. He was unconscious but breathing steadily.

Darel reached for his dagger. He needed to hop across those fifteen feet, slash a hole in the net, and drag Gee into the underbrush. All without the scorpions noticing.

His fingers closed on his dagger, the long muscles in his legs tensed . . .

"Throw the tree on the cart," Commander Pigo barked. "We're done here. We've done more than enough for the spider queen."

Darel froze as two scorpions clattered closer. They dragged the tree onto their cart, and a third scorpion grabbed the net with Gee.

"Move out!" Pigo ordered. "Double time!"

They secured the tree with leather straps, then followed a dusty trail down from the outcropping. The wooden wheels creaked, and the scorpions' many legs clattered on the ground.

Darel swallowed his dread with a loud gulp. He didn't have time to jump back to the village—and even if he did, what could anyone do to help Gee?

Nothing.

He hopped across the outcropping, almost falling into the hole where the tree had been. He caught himself, then raised his head to watch the cloud of dust from the cart drift above the hills.

Scorpion scouts and the spider queen's nightcasting were bad, but Gee being dragged away was worse. The hunting party would warn the chief about the scorps, so Darel knew exactly what *he* had to do.

"Okay," he muttered. "Don't mess this up."

With nothing but his dagger and a heart full of fear, he started tracking the scorpions. Their trail led into the ravine and up the third hill. Darel followed it easily, staying well behind the scorpions, waiting for his chance. Maybe they'd stop for a break and leave Gee alone. Maybe they'd stop for the night, and Darel could free Gee while they slept.

By the time Darel reached the top of the third hill, the sun was setting, a blood-red smear across the desert. Despite the coolness of the air, the desert seemed to radiate heat.

Or maybe that was just nerves: He was at the very edge of the Veil. Another few steps, and he'd leave the Amphibilands behind.

Darel thought about his mom saying, "I trust you." Then he started hopping . . . through the Veil, into the deadly distance.

# 15

THE PLANTS GROWING ALONG THE path were gnarled and spiky, with none of the lush green of home. At least the dusk gave Darel some cover as he followed the sound of the creaking cart.

The hills flattened into a desolate plain. The earth underfoot grew dry and cracked and turned to hard-packed dirt.

At first Darel's senses were alert to every sound and smell, his heart beating frantically and his hand twitching to his dagger every ten hops. But after an uneventful hour, he started to relax . . . and even get a little sleepy.

He continued onward, keeping himself awake with thoughts of Gee. Then with a sudden jolt of adrenaline, he realized he was hopping across a battlefield.

According to Old Jir, the dry plain just past the Outback Hills was the site of the final battle of the Hidingwar. He gazed at the barrenness. Here the

Kulipari had defeated the scorpion hordes—though the victory had driven them to near-extinction.

Here the mighty crocodiles had attacked; here the turtle king had cast the Veil. Even regular wood frog and bullfrog soldiers had taken part in that battle, supporting the Kulipari with swords and shields, with long leaps and flashing tongues.

Darel crouched and grabbed a handful of dirt, then let it slip through his finger pads. Maybe his father had stood on this very spot, single-handedly facing down a squad of charging scorpions.

And now, years later, his son was single-handedly tracking down another squad. He hoped his father would be proud of his courage rather than ashamed of his foolishness.

Darel raised his head to gaze at the stars dotting the night sky.

Then he sighed. What his father might think didn't matter at the moment. He needed to save Gee. He filled his throat with air, feeling the skin bulge, then continued onward.

As he hopped through the night, mountains loomed in the distance, and smaller hills rose closer to him. They were dotted with bushes that looked black in the moonlight. The hike was long, the trail was rough, and he was afraid he'd lose the cart. The scorpions were larger than he was and better at traveling in the outback. And Darel was thirsty. He'd need to stop for water soon.

Still, he didn't fall too far behind. He was a wood frog—what he lacked in size he made up for in determination. He'd seen his mother work through the night a hundred times, and *hopping* through the night wasn't that much different.

Heading past a stand of thorn trees, he paused to watch humped shadows in the distance: a troop of kangaroos grazing on shrubs. A short time later, a glow appeared on the far side of a looming ridge.

At first, Darel didn't understand: It was hours before dawn. Then he realized that the glow was campfires—thousands of campfires. The entire scorpion army was waiting on the other side of that ridge.

"Oh boy," he muttered, feeling his eyes bulge.

At that moment, the cart carrying the waratah tree was silhouetted at the top of the ridge.

Darel started after it—then froze. The creak of carapaces sounded from nearby, the crunch of too many scorpion feet, the jangle of battle gear.

With his eyes wide and his nostrils clenched, Darel scanned the shadow of the ridge and saw them: a two-scorp patrol walking the perimeter of the big encampment.

Heading directly for him.

Fifteen feet away.

Ten feet away.

In a sudden panic, Darel forgot all his years of practice, of stalking the bigger frogs and sneaking through the brush. He sprang backward, a high leap that sent him sprawling beside a thicket of sharp-edged grass, his heart thumping in his chest.

"You hear that?" one of the scorpions said, raising her stinger.

"Of course I heard it," the other scorp grunted. "Probably one of those scaly-foot lizards slinking around again."

Darel wriggled into the sand beneath the hillock of grass, burying himself up to his head. His ragged, frightened breathing sounded loud in his ears.

"Maybe," the first scorpion said. "I thought I saw something jump."

"Where?"

"Over there. Near that grass."

At the scraping of feet prowling closer, Darel shifted deeper, narrowed his nostrils, and prayed he was hidden.

A hard edge of something half-buried under the grass jabbed into his cheek, but he didn't move. Maybe being mud-colored would save him again.

The footsteps came closer.

Deadly pincers prodded the grass.

# 16

A RAZOR-SHARP SCORPION TAIL JAMMED into the earth an inch from Darel's shoulder, and he had to force himself to stop trembling.

The scorps kicked the hillock a few times, and then one of them grunted, "Nothing here but dirt."

A moment later, they headed off. Darel didn't dare move.

He stayed half-buried, ignoring the pain in his cheek and wrestling the fear in his mind. With patrols like that, how was he going to sneak into the camp? And once he got there, he'd stick out like a . . . well, like a frog in an army of scorpions.

If only he really *were* a sandpaper frog, he'd have the run of the camp as a mercenary. At least, according to Old Jir's stories. It was hard to imagine a frog crazy enough to wander around among a bunch of scorps.

Once he was sure the patrol was gone, Darel scrambled out of the sand and brushed the grains from his arms and legs. He felt light-headed with fear and relief. When his heartbeat returned to normal, he rubbed his aching cheek, then poked around to see what had been jabbing him.

Felt like metal. He tugged at a hard edge, and worked leather shone dully in the moonlight.

A bowl?

No, a helmet. A battered old helmet—probably from the Hidingwar. He brushed dirt from the inside, as an idea glimmered in the back of his mind.

Darel dug around a little more but didn't find anything else. So he cleaned and polished the helmet as well as he could, then tugged it onto his head.

Not a bad fit, though it smelled like dirt.

*Okay*, he told himself. *Act like a Kulipari. Act like a warrior. Get moving.*

Instead, he crouched there, slowly inflating his throat. He'd never been this frightened before. He'd always dreamed of fighting the scorpions, of glorious victories, of beating a dozen enemies single-handedly.

But the truth was that just *one* scorpion was enough to scare the warts off him. A whole army of them was a nightmare.

He wasn't sure if he could go on. Still, he knew

he couldn't run away. When he'd asked Chief Olba how you knew what was right, she'd said, "Maybe you don't."

Well, he didn't know if *this* was right, but he knew he'd never turn his back on Gee. Maybe that's what she'd meant.

So after a minute he stretched his long legs and returned to the scorpions' trail, a little wider here from traffic to the scorpion camp.

He hopped up the ridge, then paused at the top, staring at the size of the scorp encampment. The tents seemed to reach halfway to the horizon, in messy rows with openings for training grounds and fire pits. Most of them were the same size, probably barracks, but a few were larger: mess halls or armories.

And the entire place hummed with activity. Fire-light glinted off carapaces; the clash of fighting rang in the night. A bark of harsh laughter sounded. Smoke from a hundred fires blurred the moonlight and carried the scent of roasting cockroach.

He scanned the camp but didn't see the soldiers who were holding Gee.

There was no way to sneak into an army that size— which meant that he had only one way forward. Darel inflated his throat a few times, then strolled openly

along the path, trying to swagger a little like he wasn't terrified.

On the outskirts of the tents, a bunch of scorpions turned a dripping chunk of rat meat over a spit. They glanced at him but didn't say anything. They must've figured he was allowed there, because what kind of frog would wander into the scorpion horde if he didn't belong?

A *crazy* frog.

Darel almost smiled to himself, but the dark shadows and flickering fires kept his face frozen.

He checked the path, and, despite all the scuffs and bootmarks, he found faint indentations from the cart's wheels. He followed them deeper into the camp, skirting a gang of rowdy scorpion warriors.

The cart tracks disappeared at a wide intersection, but Darel found them again in the alley beyond. His eyes were bulging halfway out of his head, and he paused in the shadow of a tent to gather his courage.

Strange sounds and foreign smells swirled around him, so he did the calming exercise that Old Jir had taught him. His heart rate slowed and his hands steadied—then he glanced at the tent flap beside him.

Frogskin.

The tent was made of frogskin.

Disgust rose in his stomach and turned his nostrils to slits. And then, following the disgust, something else: anger. A hot anger that burned away his fear.

These scorpions had invaded his home. They'd kidnapped his friend. They lived in tents of frogskin, and they planned to overrun the Amphibilands and suck all the life from the forests and ponds and swamps, leaving lifeless desert behind.

No. Not without a fight. Maybe he was just a wood frog, but Chief Olba was right. Wood frogs never gave up.

Never.

# 17

AREL NARROWED HIS EYES AND continued along the wide alley between tents.

A moment later, a scorpion soldier loomed in front of him. "What're *you* doing, hopper?" the scorp growled.

Faced with eight legs, a curved stinger, protruding mouthparts, and at least five pairs of eyes, Darel froze.

Then he shook himself, like shaking water off his skin after a swim, and snarled back, "What's it look like? I'm returning to the barracks."

He kept walking, and the scorpion watched him for a second, his tail swaying in the air. Then the soldier shrugged, his eight legs shifted, and he continued on his way.

Darel managed not to faint. He knew how to act now: If he was as rude as a sandpaper frog, nobody would suspect him. As long as he didn't show fear, he'd fit right in.

So he swallowed his terror and followed the cart

tracks, getting closer and closer to a grand pavilion in the middle of the encampment. Probably the scorpion lord's tent.

And finally he found Gee.

The path opened into a wide, torchlit clearing with a circular fence in the center. It looked like a sparring ring or a place where the scorps staged gladiator fights. A few scorpions lounged at a table, gnawing on hunks of possum meat and tossing the bones into a pile on the ground.

Past them, a row of cages stood in the shadows. Whimpering sounded from the dark recesses, and as Darel edged closer, his nostrils closed at the stench of fear and hunger and sickness.

A battle net lay on the ground in front of one of the cages, and in the flickering of the torches, Darel saw a flash of brown-green skin and bulging yellow eyes—Gurnugan.

Alive and awake and terrified.

Darel almost croaked in relief. He managed to stay quiet, though, and quickly hopped toward Gee—then he stopped short. The cages were locked with thick chains, and a guard patrolled the shadows, pausing now and then to kick at the bars.

The guard was a rock lizard, a brawny mercenary

with dark stripes running along his brow that made it seem like he was scowling. Plus, he *was* scowling.

His overlapping scales looked like armor plating, and as he paced, his muscular tail dragged in the dirt behind him. No way Darel could get past him and through that chain. But he hadn't come all this way to fail with Gee in sight.

He tried to think of a plan, but he couldn't concentrate while standing in the middle of the scorpion army. He could barely remember his own name. As he stood there gulping, another lizard mercenary lumbered from the opposite side of the clearing.

"Hey, Nogo," the new arrival said to the scowling lizard. "Your shift is over."

Nogo grunted. "About time. I always get stuck guarding the cells."

"The toughest fighters stand guard." The newcomer tasted the air with her tongue. "That's why it's always you or me. Only way to get out of it is to lose a fight to one of those weaklings back at camp. You know that. Any news?"

"We got a new prisoner," Nogo growled. "Straight from the Amphibilands."

"Fresh meat."

"Not for us." Nogo scratched his scaly scalp. "Commander Pigo's saving him for Marmoo."

"So *he* can crunch the croaker's bones?"

Nogo shrugged. "Don't matter to me, long as I get paid." He kicked a cage door with his clawed foot, then turned away. "I'm heading back to camp."

Darel watched the big scowling lizard shamble along a path between two tents. He nibbled nervously on a finger pad, then realized what he had to do. He started after Nogo, walking in a bowlegged strut to make himself look more lizard-like.

A pair of grizzled scorpions brushed past him, and one jostled him with her rear legs. Darel ignored the jolt of fear and kept watching Nogo, who was weaving through the maze of frogskin and turtle-shell tents toward his own camp.

The mercenary camp. That's what Darel needed, a company of sandpaper frogs. He looked enough like one to pass—he hoped. Then at least he could blend in while he figured out how to free Gee.

He followed Nogo to the outskirts of the scorpion encampment, where a ring of tents stood at the base of a sandy hill. The rock lizard crossed a clearing, pushed through a flap, and disappeared.

Darel stopped, his eyes bulging. He didn't see frogs anywhere in the mercenary camp—just lizards. Most of them looked like monitor lizards, hard-eyed and rough-scaled.

Maybe this wasn't such a great idea after all. Maybe he should just stick close to Gee and pray for a chance.

He turned to retrace his steps when a guttural voice sounded from the shadows: "You! Croaker!"

Swallowing hard, he kept walking, hoping that the owner of the voice wouldn't follow. But he heard scuffling behind him, and a moment later a scaled paw clamped his shoulder.

"I'm talking to *you*, longlegs," the voice growled.

# 18

AREL TURNED AND FOUND himself gazing up at a brutal-looking lizard with a spiny frill. One eye gleamed red, and the other was covered with a patch. His claws curved to razor points.

"Me?" Darel squeaked.

"No," the lizard sneered sarcastically. "The croaker behind you."

"I'm looking—" Darel gulped. "Looking for the sandpaper frogs. I'm here to join the mercenaries."

"*You*, a mercenary?"

"That's right."

"You look more like a snack than a soldier."

"Oh, yeah? Well, um, er . . ." He didn't know what to say, so he just gulped again. "Um, where are the sandpapers?"

"Guarding the scorpion lord's fortress," the frilled lizard said. "Doing the grunt work, where they belong."

"Kick his warty butt, Captain Killara," another lizard called. "Show him where *he* belongs!"

The lizard captain showed Darel his sharp claws. "Okay, frog. Give me one reason I shouldn't serve you roasted with onions."

"I'll give you two reasons," Darel blurted. "First, I can beat any new recruit you've got. And second—"

A hiss of laughter sounded from the fire pit. "Scrawny frog. I could whip you with one claw tied behind my back."

Darel peered into the firelight and saw a three-toed skink. "How about you put your scales where your mouth is?" he said, trying to sound tough.

To his relief, the lizard captain lowered his clawed hand. But then said, "That might liven up the evening." Killara gave a wicked grin. "Let's see you two fight. If you win, frog, we won't eat you—at least not tonight."

Two minutes later, Darel found himself circling the skink as the other lizards crowded around, jeering and spitting. What was he *doing*? He couldn't beat a real warrior.

Darel's eyes bulged as he warily watched the skink, waiting for him to make the first move.

They circled twice, and the jeers from the crowd grew louder. The skink was long and sinuous, with stubby, muscular arms and legs and a mean glint in his eyes. He moved smoothly, his long body relaxed and ready.

Then he attacked. He seemed to uncoil, his body twice as long as it looked, and his scaly fist flashed at Darel. The young frog leaped desperately backward, twisting to avoid the blow—and slammed to the ground, his legs curled tight to his chest.

When the skink rushed him again, claws extended, Darel tried to shove him away, but the skink easily brushed his hands aside.

That's when Darel flicked his tongue at the skink's eyes.

The skink jerked backward, and Darel kicked his powerful legs. The skink wasn't the only one who was longer than he looked—Darel's right foot caught the skink in his chest . . . hard.

The skink went flying into the air, his body squirming. He sailed over the crowd of onlookers, who grunted and laughed. Then he crashed into a tent, tearing a hole in the side.

Darel stood, brushed dirt from his legs, and made a sour face. The skink tasted disgusting. But he'd done it. He'd won.

Nothing happened—for a moment. Then a big paw

appeared in the hole that the skink had torn in the tent.
Followed by a big head. And Nogo stepped through,
his scowl even angrier.

He glared at the crowd. "Who woke me?"

"The frog," somebody squeaked.

"Take care of him," Captain Killara told the big rock lizard.

Nogo shoved through the crowd toward Darel. He looked like an angry mountain with claws and a tail.

Darel nervously inflated his throat. He'd *barely* beaten the skink—Nogo was too big and strong for him.

But he couldn't run. If he ran now, he'd have to keep running all the way back to the Amphibilands— and leave Gee behind.

So he took a shaky breath and faced the big rock lizard.

There was no circling, no wary testing.

Instead, Nogo simply lumbered toward him.

Darel planted his feet the way Old Jir had taught him and, drawing on years of practice, punched the big lizard as hard as he could.

Nogo didn't seem to notice.

Instead, he swung one of his big claws. Darel saw a scaly blur, then felt the impact against his cheek. The campfire flickered and the lizards' voices hushed. Darel hit the ground, and darkness fell.

# 19

OMETHING STANK LIKE ROTTEN vegetables and stagnant marsh water. Pain throbbed in time with Darel's heartbeat—mostly in his head and arm. After a time, he realized that he was croaking, a low, sad chorus of one.

So he quieted and opened his eyes. Kangaroo hide stretched above him, and smoke was thick in the air.

He was lying on a cot inside a long rectangular tent. Dozens of cots lined each wall, with footlockers beside them. A row of thick poles marched down the center of the tent, and a few small fires smoldered in pits beneath blackened copper pots. Soiled clothing draped over cots, and trash was scattered everywhere.

Lizards snored in the smoky half-light, a hissing wheeze that set Darel's teeth on edge. A sudden fear struck him, and he reached for his belt, sure that the lizards had stolen his dagger. But, no, the hilt rested comfortably in his palm, and he inflated his throat in relief.

The relief didn't last long.

A guttural voice suddenly sounded behind him. "I've got a question for you, croaker."

He started like a surprised tree frog, then turned. Captain Killara sat on the next cot, watching him with his one reddish eye.

Darel suppressed a shudder of fear. "Oh, um— yes?"

"You said there were two reasons I shouldn't serve you roasted with onions. One was because you could beat my recruits. What was the other?"

"Because I'd taste better in a cream sauce."

The captain grunted—not quite a laugh, but close. "You've got guts, croaker, I'll give you that. You're fast, too."

Darel rubbed his aching head, reminding himself to act tough and unafraid. "Not fast enough," he said. "The sandpaper frogs really aren't here?"

The captain nodded. "That's why you came, huh? To enlist?"

"Sure," Darel said. "I mean, why else would a frog come to the scorpion camp?"

"Good question." The captain's eye narrowed. "You don't mind fighting your own kind?"

Darel tried a mean smile. "Not if I'm getting paid."

"In that case, I could use a frog like you. Small and mud-green—makes you good for scouting."

"How much?" Darel asked.

The captain explained the pay and the duties involved, but Darel only half-listened, his mind on Gee.

So he nodded, even when Killara said, ". . . your job is to clean the tents, do the laundry, polish the gear. And stay out of everyone's way. Do that well enough, and we'll see about training you to scout."

"Hey, bosss," a slithery voice said from across the tent. "Did you jussst tell the croaker to clean for usss?"

"That's right."

The lizard shoved some dirty clothes to the floor. "Then clean thisss, frog."

"And that," a broad-shouldered monitor lizard said, gesturing to a pile of dirty dishes. "I'm tired of eating off crusty plates."

"And make my bed," a third lizard snarled, from a few cots down.

"And mine," another voice said.

Darel gulped in dismay as a chorus of gruff, hissing voices filled the tent. So much for his daydreams of battle and victory. Even after bravely sneaking into the scorp camp and joining a mercenary company, he was still stuck doing the cleaning.

# 20

CHIEF OLBA'S THROAT WAS BULGING as she hopped into the Outback Hills. She paused in the shade of a cotton bush to catch her breath, and a dozen frogs waited with her: grizzled old veterans who hadn't carried a spear since the Hidingwar, a few of the more proficient hunters, and the healer, along with his daughter, Coorah. Even Arabanoo, the white-lipped tree frog, had come along—though Olba guessed that he was mostly interested in impressing Coorah.

She gazed at the assembled frogs. They were all willing to fight, but even the veterans were farmers and merchants at heart, not warriors.

Coorah offered her a gourd. "Want a sip of water, chief? It's good for digestion."

"Digestion is the one thing I *don't* have trouble with."

"It's lime flavored, too."

"In that case," Olba said, smiling her thanks, "how can I resist?"

She drank, then sprinkled some water on the glossy skin of her forehead. She always thought best when slightly moistened.

The top of the first hill was only a hundred yards away. Perhaps she'd find some answers there. If the story about scorpions inside the Veil was true, the Amphibilands was in deadly peril.

And what else would explain Darel and Gurnu-gun's disappearance days earlier?

She furrowed her brow as she resumed the climb. When Darel and Gurnugan hadn't returned that first evening, everyone assumed the two young friends were off on an adventure.

Then the hunters arrived, telling a wild tale of scorpions in the Outback Hills, attacking them and kidnapping Gurnugan. They'd spent the entire night looking but found no further sign of the scorps *or* the froglings.

Search parties were scouring the eucalyptus forest, but the chief had decided to travel to the hills herself. If the Veil was falling, she had to prepare the frogs. They were in grave danger.

"There!" Coorah said, pointing toward a wattle-flower bush. "Some of the flowers are freshly cut."

"So we know they got this far," Olba said.

"This is all my fault!" Coorah croaked. "If I hadn't asked for the flowers, Darel and Gee—"

"Nonsense," Chief Olba snapped. "*If* anything happened, it's nobody's fault but the scorpions'! And why did you want the flowers?"

"To make medicine—a better way to treat wounds."

"That's right, because you and Darel were the only ones who saw this coming." Olba raised her voice.

"Chief!" one of the hunters called. "Here—look."

Olba hopped closer and inspected the ground.

Her inner eyelids flickered in dismay. There could be no mistake. Here, in the dirt of the Outback Hills, were the tracks of a scorpion warrior.

"*Inside* the Veil," someone gasped.

"Impossible," someone else muttered. "If they're inside the Veil, we're dead. We're all dead."

"Let's continue," Olba said, before the fear spread. "Follow the boys' footprints. Stay alert, everyone."

The hunters searched through the underbrush until they reached the top of the first hill, where the lead hunter said, "They stopped here. Gurnugan turned back, and Darel continued to the second hill."

"Why'd they stop?"

"Because . . ." Coorah's voice shook as she pointed into the distance. "Chief, over there."

In the desert beyond the Outback Hills, the scorpion army covered the dunes like spines on an echidna.

"There's more of them than in the Hidingwar," Olba gasped, her eyes bulging.

"Twice as many," an old veteran muttered. "And we've got no Kulipari."

For a long moment, Olba didn't speak. Then she puffed her throat and said, "We need to tell the turtle king. He's the only one who can save us."

"But—" Coorah shook her head. "There's an army between us and the Turtle Coves."

"Someone will need to sneak past."

"That's suicide," the old veteran said.

"But if we don't reach the turtle king," Chief Olba said, "we're dead . . . We're dead either way."

"We'll do it," Arabanoo said. "Me and my friends. We'll do it."

Olba smiled at him—a little sadly. "That's brave, Arabanoo, but you're barely more than froglings."

"That's right," Coorah's father said. "We need to send our best hunters. We need frogs who were in the war and still remember how to fight."

"What we need," Chief Olba said, "is a chorus."

After they returned to the village, Chief Olba gathered frogs from every village and tree and burrow in the meeting hall.

She told them about the scorpions in the Outback Hills and the army gathering in the desert beyond. A frightened croaking filled the hall—the echoing ribbet of the burrowers, the musical call of the peepers, the low rasp of the Baw Baws.

Olba asked for quiet. "We need volunteers," she croaked, "to leave the safety of the Amphibilands and travel to the turtle king, to ask for his help."

"How're they supposed to get around the scorpion army?" Old Jir asked, leaning on his cane.

"I don't know," the chief answered. "They'll have to sneak past without being seen."

"Impossible!" a burly bullfrog called, her lumpy face scowling. "Maybe you saw scorp tracks in the Hills, but we're still safe *here*."

"Not for long," Old Jir croaked.

"The Veil will protect us!" the bullfrog rumbled. "We're panicking over nothing."

"That's why I called this chorus." Olba looked over the crowd. "We must decide what to do. Arm ourselves? Hope the Veil holds? Or ask for volunteers to alert the turtle king?"

A few tree frogs shouted, "Arm ourselves!"

From a shadowed burrow, a low voice said, "Warn the king."

"Do nothing," the burly bullfrog rumbled.

A moment later, other frogs started repeating those phrases—*Arm ourselves ... Warn the king ... Do nothing* ... Soon a chorus of croaking filled the meeting hall.

At first, *Do nothing* drowned out the other phrases, and Olba's forehead furrowed deeply.

Then, slowly but steadily, *Warn the king* grew louder and louder. Within minutes, all the frogs were chanting together, *Warn the king, Warn the king*, and the cry shook the walls and echoed above the village.

Then the chorus stopped, and Chief Olba spoke into the sudden quiet: "We will need volunteers— experienced trackers and fighters. This is a dangerous job. You might not survive. But you must try."

After a moment, the burly bullfrog hopped forward. "I'll go."

"Me too," a tree frog said, leaping down from the branches.

Soon, five of the best hunters in the Amphibilands had volunteered, frogs who could put an arrow in a snake's eye and track a butterfly across a lake. They were joined by four middle-aged veterans of the Hidingwar, who would now take their dusty shields from chests and strap themselves into creaking armor.

Early the next day, the village arranged a send-off at the edge of the Veil.

The party of courageous frogs set off—braving the scorpion army, risking unknown dangers. Olba watched them leave, a weight in her heart. So much depended on their success.

The following morning, an urgent croaking woke her from restless sleep. She found a grim-faced frog outside her door.

"Bad news," he told her.

Olba swallowed. "What happened?"

"A scorpion war party found them, chased them back here. Of the nine volunteers, only two survived. There's no way to reach the turtle king."

Olba made a soft, mournful croak. "Oh, those poor, brave frogs."

"What are we going to do now?" the grim-faced frog asked.

"What *can* we do?" she said. "Prepare for the worst."

# 21

LORD MARMOO PACED THE FLOORS OF the rocky chamber, his eight-legged stride clattering against the stone. He didn't like the spider queen's castle— the cramped corridors, the moist air, the weight of the boulders around him. Give him the harsh desert sands, the burning sun high overhead, and the scorched air.

Still, he needed Queen Jarrah—just as she needed him—so he'd tolerate the discomfort. He'd tolerate a great deal more than discomfort if it helped him conquer the Amphibilands and claim all that fresh water and easy prey for his scorpion nation.

Only then would he turn his attention to the spiders.

"Soon," he told himself. "Soon that day will come."

He turned suddenly and marched down the corridor. He crossed the web moat, heading for the mines. He didn't know if Jarrah mined gems for her nightcasting or simply because she liked jewelry, but he hadn't killed anything in days; perhaps he'd sink his stinger into some scrawny miner.

Killing always improved his mood.

But halfway to the mines, he found something even better: Commander Pigo and a company of soldiers, coming from the desert encampment with an Amphibilands tree for the spider queen.

"Pigo," he said, scuttling closer. "Report in."

"Everything went according to plan, my lord. We uprooted the tree and withdrew. We even captured a succulent frog."

"Well done, little brother. A well-deserved meal for me when I return from this wretched place."

Pigo saluted crisply. "Your troops are assembled, my lord, and eager to crush the croakers. They wait only for your command."

"And I wait only for the spider queen," Marmoo said.

Together, they delivered the tree to Queen Jarrah, who was lounging with her ladies-in-waiting at the top of her boulder castle.

"This is from inside the Amphibilands?" she asked.

Marmoo nodded, his main eyes bright and his side eyes watchful. "From the Outback Hills."

"Then the Veil will soon fall—as I promised."

"And I will lure the turtle king from his Coves—as I promised."

"Excellent," she said. "The old fool cannot even sense how strong I've become. But an attack on his precious frogs should rouse him."

Jarrah circled the tree, stroking each of the bright red flowers in turn. Then she stopped abruptly at the single white bloom, a big flower head with rings of little petals.

"Perfect," she murmured. "Look how lovely and glowing and pure."

She called her ladies closer, and they surrounded the uprooted waratah tree. Each pulled a strand of webbing from her spinnerets, and then Queen Jarrah began nightcasting.

Her eyes shone black as she summoned her poison. The silk shimmered and twisted.

A noxious cloud rose above the writhing web, and Jarrah stared into the smoke as her long legs danced across the silken strands, plucking and tugging and strumming.

The cloud seemed to pulse with power. Marmoo had heard that dreamcasting was a quiet magic, almost like meditation, but this was something completely different. Watching Jarrah tap into her full night-casting strength, he finally saw why she hated the turtle king so much.

Sergu used thoughts and visions to propel his power forward, like a turtle gliding through the ocean, riding the currents. Jarrah, on the other claw, used her silken web and poison fangs to trap her power, to drain magical energy from the world, like sucking blood from a fly.

Marmoo realized she hated King Sergu because he reminded her that without him and his stupid, gentle magic, she could never have invented nightcasting. Without his lessons, she would've remained an ordinary spider—and died long ago. She owed her life and her power to the magic she despised.

Of course, she'd taken all his lessons and turned them upside-down. She'd turned dreamcasting into a *weapon*.

Marmoo smiled to himself, grinding his mouthparts in appreciation as he watched her work.

Finally, a strand of her web snapped, and he felt an eerie pulse through the windless day, as if the air had suddenly thickened around him.

The white flower turned to ash, and the rest of the waratah tree shriveled into a handful of blackened twigs. Jarrah lowered her arms and swayed, exhausted from her nightcasting. She sank her fangs into a silken bundle her attendants provided.

After she drained the blood, she sighed deeply.

"Success?" Marmoo asked, his pincers clenching expectantly.

"Indeed, Lord Marmoo," she purred. "I've learned exactly how to undo the turtle king's feeble magic. Take me within the outermost layer of the Veil, and I will destroy it completely in a day."

"Then we'll leave immediately."

Jarrah wagged her finger at him. "My lord—there's no reason for such unseemly haste."

Marmoo heard the iron in her voice, despite her teasing tone, and realized his error. If she thought he was trying to rush her, she'd slow down, just to prove that she wasn't in his control.

He gave a courtly bow with his mid-legs and said, "Of course, Queen Jarrah. Excuse my impatience. I'm simply eager to present your gift."

She brightened with interest. "My gift?"

"Waiting for you at the encampment. My soldiers captured a frog inside the Amphibilands, plump and juicy, with smooth, shiny skin. We're keeping him in a cage for you, to give you the honor of the first taste of Amphibilands frog."

She laughed, a tinkling sound like glass breaking. "Then, by all means, I will pack as quickly as I can. Why, I can taste him already!"

## 22

AREL'S FIFTH MORNING IN THE mercenary camp started the same as the first four.

He woke before any of the lizards and checked his ratty old shield and armor—and of course the dagger that never left his hip. Then he grabbed a ladle of mush from the common pot and stuffed his face, trying not to taste the food. He was eating for strength, not for flavor.

He stretched and practiced the drills that the grizzled lizard trainer had showed him and then went for a run—in full armor, looking more like a lizard than a frog.

Every morning, he hopped past the cages where they kept Gee, and every morning a lizard was on duty, watchful as a hungry hawk. And to make things worse, the captain only assigned the toughest lizards, the ones who'd won spars, to guard duty.

When Darel returned to the mercenary camp, he scrubbed the floors and scoured the dishes. He polished armor and hauled the trash to the pit. Then he did the laundry, and when he got back from that, the dishes were dirty again. Then he made the cots, tidied the tent, and swept the floors one more time.

The lizards thought they were grinding him down with all the chores, but they didn't know his secret: He was his mother's hardworking son. He pretended he was exhausted in the evenings and slumped down at the sparring pit, watching the fights—but actually, he'd hardly broken a sweat.

No one could work harder than a wood frog.

He liked spending the evenings watching the mercenaries fight, seeing the different styles, then practicing the new moves himself. He watched the scorpions, too. They sparred viciously, tails slashing and pincers snapping. And unlike the lizards, the scorps sometimes fought to the death. A victorious scorpion would strike his opponent in the only weak spot, the unprotected underbelly.

When Darel first saw that, his nostrils had slitted in satisfaction. The tales were true. Those tough scorpion carapaces had one major vulnerability.

Plus, he'd seen proof of what Old Jir had told him. Scorps always obeyed the strongest scorpion. If a squad leader lost a fight, the squad members milled around in confusion for a while, then wandered away. They didn't know how to think for themselves.

And they simply weren't curious. Darel had spent four days in the camp without raising suspicions. Scorpions just didn't have the imagination to wonder about him.

The morning of the fifth day, though, something changed.

Darel jumped through the sprawling encampment toward Gee's cage. He hopped into the clearing, then paused at the table where sleepy scorpions crunched on crickets every morning.

Except this morning they stood in an alert line, and a new scorpion squad had claimed the table.

The new scorpions weren't bigger than the others, but something about them made Darel nervous.

They wore wide red bands around their tails and moved with a quiet, predatory confidence. And when he jumped into the clearing, all six of them shifted toward him, their legs scuttling.

"You," one of them rasped. "Frog."

"Yeah?" he said, using his best mercenary voice.

"Come closer . . ."

He hopped toward them, his throat puffing nervously. "You want something?"

The scorpion narrowed her main eyes. "We want to know why your webbed feet are befouling Lord Marmoo's encampment."

"I'm with Captain Killara's mercenary company."

"You're no lizard." The red-banded scorpion's mouthparts ground together. "You smell like the other frog."

"What other frog?"

The scorpion gave a rough laugh. "The one in the cage. You smell like him. Not of desert. Of eucalyptus trees and moist places."

"You want to know why?" Darel asked, hoping they couldn't hear the terrified beating of his heart. "Because I'm not a scorpion. I bathe."

The red-banded scorpion twitched, and her stinger sliced through the air and stopped inches from Darel's face. Quivering and dripping with poison. "Watch your tongue," she said. "Or I'll cut your throat."

Darel gulped, and his inner eyelids blinked rapidly. These red-banded scorpions were even deadlier than Nogo, who'd knocked him out without trying.

"Perhaps we should kill you anyway," the scorpion continued. "And give the spider queen two gifts."

"W-w-what do you mean?"

"The other frog." The scorpion's side eyes glanced toward Gee's cage. "He's a present for Queen Jarrah. She's getting the first taste of Amphibilands frog."

"But not the last!" another scorpion said.

"She's coming to wrap that fat frog in her silk," the first red-banded scorpion continued. "She'll suck his blood for a midnight snack, then tear down the Veil, and we'll march."

"Oh," Darel said, weakly. "Good."

"Looking forward to the battle, are you?"

"Yeah. Tear down the Veil and"—he felt a little dizzy—"and invade. When, um . . . when's she coming?"

"Why? You want to watch her eat frog flesh?" The scorpion laughed. "She'll get here tonight. She'll have her snack, and tomorrow the Amphibilands will fall."

"In that case, I should . . . um, polish my shield."

"You do that, little pollywog. And take care. Because tomorrow night, you'll be among the last of your kind."

As the scorpions chuckled, Darel hopped across the clearing, a little unsteadily.

The lizard guarding the cages saw him and muttered, "Don't mess with those scorps. They're elite troopers. Tougher than crocodile hide."

"Yeah," Darel said. "I noticed."

He started back toward the barracks, lost in thought. The spider queen was coming, to eat Gee tonight and destroy the Veil tomorrow. He needed to do something—but what?

At the mercenary camp again, Darel leaned against the railing that surrounded the sparring pit, a twenty-foot-deep hole in the sandy ground. Bits of dented armor were stacked against the railing beside him, and he absently fingered a heavy copper shield.

A few of the other mercenaries shouted insults at him, but he ignored them. He didn't need to practice fighting. He needed to think of a plan.

# 23

ROG!" CAPTAIN KILLARA BELLOWED from inside his tent. "Get your skinny green butt in here!"

Darel narrowed his nostrils wearily and pushed into the captain's tent. He found the one-eyed lizard sitting at a desk poring over maps, with huge Nogo standing beside him.

"Yes, sir?" he asked.

"We're marching tomorrow, frog. Lord Marmoo's putting our company in front."

"Shock troops," Nogo muttered, scratching his scaly neck with one claw.

"What does that mean?" Darel asked.

"Means we go in first and get hit hardest," Killara told him. "That's why they pay us."

"Oh."

"Of course, the scorps only paid us to breach the hills." The captain's tongue flicked in disgust. "Only paid us to *start* the fight, not *finish* it."

Nogo hissed. "Cheap eight-legs."

"Yeah, they'll expect us to burn the forests and villages, even though they haven't paid for anything past the first battle." Killara rubbed his eye. "They always want more than they pay for."

"So we're the shock troops?" Darel said.

"Not you." Captain Killara fixed Darel with a slitted gaze. "You'll go in first and scout the area."

"Yes, sir."

The captain turned to the big rock lizard. "Time to get to the prison cages, Nogo. You're on guard duty."

"Again?" Nogo grumbled. "I ought to have the day off if I'm leading the fight tomorrow."

Killara snorted. "The only way you get a break is if someone whips you in the sparring pit. Then *he* can guard the cells while you're healing."

"Guess I'm stuck guarding, then." Nogo's scaly mouth lifted in a grin. "Ain't a lizard in this company who can lay a paw on me."

The captain dismissed them, and Darel followed Nogo from the tent, his mind a whirl of possibility. All of a sudden, he knew what he needed to do. He needed to beat Nogo and take over his guard duty. But five days ago, the rock lizard had knocked him out without even trying.

How could he possibly win a rematch?

Only one way to find out.

So he said, "You're right that no lizard in the company can whip you."

Nogo grunted and started lumbering away.

"But *I*," Darel continued, his eyes bulging slightly, "can beat you like an egg."

A hush fell over the area.

The big lizard turned and glared down at Darel. "*You*, little frog?"

"That's right," Darel said, swallowing his uncertainty. "You're strong, but you're slow."

Nogo glowered. "Fast enough to crush you."

"And you smell like a swamp rat. I'll pluck your scales and use 'em for fly traps. And look at your stubby little bunny-rabbit tail. Can't you grow it back—"

Nogo didn't even wait to enter the sparring pit. He just bellowed and charged, his fangs bared and the razor points of his claws glinting.

Darel sprang upward, his feet inches above the slicing claws. He slapped one palm on the big lizard's head and cartwheeled in the air, landing on his feet behind Nogo.

He punched Nogo's back as hard as he could, but the lizard's scales deflected his blow.

Nogo's tail slammed the ground with a thunderous

thud, and he pivoted, his huge claw flashing toward Darel.

Darel sidestepped, then hopped backward. "See? You're slow as a lazy snail."

Despite his mockery, he knew he couldn't last long against Nogo. The lizard barely noticed his punches, and any one of Nogo's swipes would knock him into next week.

So he faked a yawn, trying to make Nogo angry and reckless, and crouched again, ready to spring.

Nogo stampeded closer, bellowing—then swung, surprisingly fast for a lizard his size.

Darel moved faster. Instead of leaping over Nogo, he sprang to the side, just ahead of the sharp claws. His toe pads helped him stick to the outside railing of the sparring pit, and the big lizard spun in a half circle, dragged by the weight of his swing.

"Ha!" Darel crowed. "Are we dancing or fighting?"

Nogo roared. "I'm gonna tear you in two!"

"Gotta catch me first," Darel said, with a bold grin.

The grin died when he tried to step away from the railing and discovered that his foot was lodged between two slats.

He tugged, but he couldn't move his leg.

He was stuck.

Nogo's tongue flicked triumphantly. "I'll snap that off for you, greenie."

"You couldn't snap a daisy without—"

Nogo charged. His feet slammed the ground, and his tail dug a furrow behind him.

He gave a mighty swipe, aiming at the center of Darel's head.

Nogo's claw was slashing toward him, and Darel didn't have time to jump away. Instead, he fell backward into the sparring pit, dropping halfway down before the slats snaring his ankle caught him.

He dangled upside down, his pulse racing, clamping his mouth shut so he couldn't croak "I surrender!"

And Nogo—unable to stop his furious blow—smashed through the railing and crashed to the bottom of the fighting pit.

With the railing broken, Darel managed to free himself and hop to the ground, bruised and breathless.

Nogo was in worse shape, moaning in a heap in the pit—but still conscious. Still able to report to guard duty.

So Darel grabbed the heavy copper shield and

leaped into the air, as high as he could. For a moment, he found himself above the scorpion encampment. He saw the tents spreading in every direction, and then he swung the shield below him and fell, fast and straight as an arrow.

He landed shield-first on the back of Nogo's head.

The clang echoed in the fighting pit, like a heavy club hitting a gong. The impact jarred Darel so hard, he flopped to his side, the wind knocked out of him.

But at last, Nogo stopped moving.

Darel struggled to his feet. He puffed his throat a few times, then climbed from the sparring pit.

The lizard mercenaries eyed him warily, and the three-toed skink muttered, "Beginner's luck."

Instead of replying, Darel flopped to the ground to catch his breath.

A minute later, Captain Killara emerged from his tent. "Where's that little croaker?" He stomped over to Darel. "You beat Nogo?"

"He's clumsy." Darel showed the captain a cheeky grin. "He beat himself."

"Well, congratulations. You just assigned yourself guard duty."

"What? No—I'm not on duty. I'm going to take a nap."

"That's what you think. You whipped Nogo, so you get his job."

Darel sighed. "Aw, captain . . ."

"Don't whine, frog. Report to the cages immediately."

"Yes, sir," he said. He grabbed a spear and hopped slowly away, hiding his smile.

# 24

AREL STOOD SENTRY OUTSIDE the cages. After days in the scorpion camp, he hardly noticed the stench or the squads of scorpions scuttling past—though he was relieved that those red-banded scorps weren't at the nearby table.

He sidled up to Gee's cage. Without moving his mouth, he said, "Ssst!"

No answer from the darkness beyond the iron bars.

He tried again. "Sssst!"

A scorpion across the clearing glanced at him with her side eyes, and Darel hopped away from the cage.

He rattled the next door, pretending to check that it was locked but actually eyeing the chain. Sentries weren't given keys, so he'd grabbed a heavy spear to help him snap the chain. Except that would make too much noise. He needed to break Gee free without the scorps noticing, and get away before the spider queen arrived for her "gift."

Darel hopped along the row of cages for a minute, then stopped again outside Gee's door. "Hey!" he hissed into the darkness. "Frog!"

A scratching sounded from inside, then a cough.

*Gee's* cough!

Darel almost peeped for joy but managed to keep scowling. "Don't say a word," he snarled. "You web-toed, mud-colored, snail-eating, wattleflower-sniffing croaker. You wart-faced son-of-a-builder! You—"

"*What?*" Gee's voice croaked from the darkness. "Is that you?"

"What do you think, web-toes?" Darel growled, then murmured: "They're watching, so keep quiet."

"Darel," Gee whispered. "What are you *doing* here?"

Darel leaned against the bars. "What do you think I'm doing?" he said without moving his lips. "I'm saving you."

"Well, stop! Run away quick, before they see you."

"They know I'm here," Darel muttered. "I joined the mercenaries."

"You *what*? You joined the *what*? You're crazy, you're nuts. You've lost your marbles, you've gone round the bend, you're—"

A squad of scorps skittered into the clearing, and Darel's inner eyelids blinked. "Shhh!" he hissed. "Back in a second."

He ambled past the other cages, acting like just another mercenary on guard duty. He scratched his forehead with a finger pad. Kicked the dirt. Puffed his throat to keep himself calm.

Then, after the squad disappeared, he returned to Gee's cage.

"—loopier than a dizzy dragonfly!" Gee was saying. "Nuttier than squirrel soup. You joined the *mercenaries*?"

"That was the only way."

Gee hopped closer to the bars, and his face looked dirty and desperate. "You've got to get out of here, Darel."

"Just as soon as I break you free."

"There's no way. Save yourself. I—I can't believe you snuck into a scorpion camp for me!" For a moment, a grin rose on Gee's face. "But you've got to leave before they catch you."

"If we don't escape, the spider queen is going to eat you," Darel said. "Tonight."

"*Eat* me?" Gee grabbed the cage bars. "Then stop messing around and get me outta here! What's the plan?"

"We'll wait until nobody's looking, and then I'll snap the chain with my spear."

"*That's* your plan?"

"Um, yeah."

"It'll take you an hour to snap this chain." Gee tapped his finger pads against the bars. "How about this? Slip me your dagger, and I'll weaken the chain on this side. Then you can snap it in a second."

"Huh," Darel said. "You know, that actually makes sense."

"Hey, I didn't listen to my parents talk about construction every day of my life without learning a few things."

Darel almost laughed. He waited until more scorpions crossed the clearing to a food cart, then slipped his dagger into the cage.

"I'd better start acting like a sentry," he whispered. "So nobody gets suspicious."

"I'll start working on the chain. And, Darel?"

"Yeah?"

"You know how everyone in the village yells at you for stirring up trouble?"

Darel paused. "Yeah?"

"What they don't realize," Gee said, a quaver in his voice, "is that you'd do anything to help your friends.

I can't believe you hopped into the middle of the scorpion army. Thanks, Darel. Just . . . thanks."

Darel blinked back tears. "Well, I couldn't let the spider queen eat you."

"Would you stop *saying* that?" Gee said with a shudder. Then he went back to working on the chain.

Darel paced in front of the cages, pausing occasionally to kick at a door to cover the sound of Gee weakening the links. He traded insults with a one-armed monitor lizard, then watched the blacksmith's cart trundle past.

Twenty minutes later, he bought some emu jerky from a vendor and slipped it to Gee along with his canteen.

All around him, the scorpion camp bustled with urgency. Everyone knew that Lord Marmoo was returning with the spider queen—and that she'd destroy the Veil. *Tomorrow*, they murmured. *Tomorrow we'll feast.*

Soldiers marched double time across the clearing, officers reviewed their orders, cooks threw rats and crickets into bubbling cauldrons. And finally, for one brief moment, Darel was alone.

In a flash, he hopped to Gee's cage and jammed his spear between the chain and the cage bars. "Get ready," he said.

He gripped the spear tightly and heaved with his legs against the bars. For a second, nothing happened. He strained and shoved—then, with a sudden *crack*, the chain snapped.

Darel staggered backward, and the cell door flew open.

Gee stumbled from the darkness. He looked terrible, with a black eye and dirty skin—and he was skinny.

Well, *almost* skinny.

Well, skinni*er*.

As Darel grabbed the spear, Gee closed the cage door and looped the broken chain through the bars, to hide the signs of his escape. He handed Darel his dagger back.

"This way," Darel said, and they hopped into a cramped passageway between two tents. "I hid some armor around the corner."

"What am I going to do with armor?" Gee asked.

"Pretend to be a mercenary. C'mon, hurry!"

"I'm . . . hurrying," Gee said, panting.

Darel glanced at Gee and saw that he was stooped over from days in the cage. "I'm sorry, Gee, I should slow down. You're hurt."

"I'm okay." Gee blinked his inner eyelids. "I just . . . What's your plan?"

"Walk out of the camp wearing armor and run for the Amphibilands."

"We can't."

"Sure, we can!" Darel insisted. "I can bluff my way past these scorps, no problem."

"It's not that." Gee put his hands on his knees and puffed his throat a few times, catching his breath. "Someone needs to warn the turtle king. I heard the scorpions talking. The spider queen's going to tear down the Veil. We need to warn King Sergu."

Darel eyed his hunched, filthy friend. "You want to hop to the Turtle Coves? You're too weak from that cage; you'll never make it."

"I spent my entire childhood chasing my crazy friend around the Amphibilands." Gee grinned suddenly, and his bulging eyes seemed to clear. "I'm tougher than I look."

"You look as tough as a wallaby's sneeze. We should head home."

"Which way are the Coves?"

Darel pointed. "Just north of here. Past the mangrove swamp, on the coast."

"Then that's where we're going."

Darel stared at Gee, impressed. "After five days in a prison cell, you want to leap across the desert and through the swamp?"

"We have to."

"Wow." Darel saw courage in his friend that he'd never noticed before. It made him feel suddenly uncertain about himself—he had always been the one who pushed for the more daring plan.

Gee held his gaze, then smiled his old goofy smile. "Well, I also heard that fat, juicy caterpillars grow on trees in the Coves, and the beach is soft as a lily pad."

Darel snorted. "It's too dangerous, Gee. You've gone through enough and . . . and I need to make sure you're safe."

"This is bigger than me, Darel," Gee said, his voice only a little shaky. "The whole Amphibilands is depending on us."

"Well, when we get back, we'll tell the chief to send someone to the turtles." Darel led Gee down another passageway. "The armor's just around the next corner. We'll—"

Three scorpion warriors stepped from a tent flap directly in front of them, and the biggest scorp snarled, "What do you think *you're* doing?"

For a second, Darel's mind blanked. Then he said, "Taking the prisoner to the laundry."

"Why?"

Darel scowled. "What do *you* care?"

"Because if I don't like your answer, I'll sting you in the eye."

"I'm going to scrub the grime off him." Darel shoved Gee. "Lord Marmoo isn't giving the spider queen a snack that smells like *this*."

The scorpion's side eyes narrowed in suspicion.

"Something doesn't look right. Take that frog back to his cage."

Darel shrugged. "Sure. But what's your name? So I can tell Lord Marmoo you said it's okay if his gift stinks. He probably won't mind."

The big scorpion's middle legs shuffled uneasily. "Fine, scrub him, then. Just be quick about it."

Darel prodded Gee with the side of his spear. "Get moving, croaker."

He marched Gee along two narrow alleys and around a corner, where they slumped in relief.

"That was close," Gee said.

"Yeah, and we can't get the armor now."

"So what do we do?"

Darel scratched his forehead thoughtfully. He wanted to race for the Turtle Coves to warn the king, but he'd promised his mother that he'd look after Gee. He'd promised Gee's father that nothing would happen. He couldn't endanger Gee, not after he'd just saved him.

"We sneak out of camp," Darel finally said. "Then we leap for the Outback Hills."

# 25

OMMANDER PIGO CRESTED THE hill, followed by dozens of Queen Jarrah's spider troops—though the queen herself traveled more slowly, in her fancy silken litter. He saw the encampment, the mightiest scorpion army in generations, and clicked his mouthparts in satisfaction.

Once in the camp, he mounted a platform in the central square to make an announcement. "Lord Marmoo and Queen Jarrah are mere hours behind me, and we're going to give them a welcome fit for royalty! Get to work, you lazy scorplings!"

Scorpions skittered away to do his bidding, and he marched among them. "Widen this path! Clear a place for the queen's tent. Clean yourself up—are you scorpions or sand fleas?"

Tent poles were straightened and pincers cleaned and black carapaces polished. The spider servants wove a silvery tent of fine webbing for Queen Jarrah.

As the camp grew tidier, Pigo remembered the

pudgy frog that Lord Marmoo was presenting to the queen. He crossed to the cages, then frowned. "Where's the guard?"

"Which guard, sir?" one of the soldiers nearby asked.

"The one watching the prisoners." He peered at the cage where the frog was kept. "Croaker! Show your face. Don't make me come in there after you."

More silence. Pigo slammed the cage door with his pincer—and the chain unwrapped from the bars and coiled at his feet.

Broken.

Snapped.

For a moment, he simply stared. Then he flung open the door and lunged inside. Empty. The gift for Queen Jarrah had escaped.

"Get me an elite squad!" he bellowed. "On the double!"

His escort scattered, and Pigo questioned the soldiers who had been sitting at the table nearby. One of them said, "The lizards were guarding the cages, sir. Well, them and that frog."

"What frog?"

"A sandpaper frog, I guess. He works for Captain Killara."

Pigo felt his stinger quiver with the urge to strike. "You're telling me that a *frog* did this?"

The soldier cowered. "I—I guess so, sir."

Pigo spun away, half-blind with fury. Some soft-skinned croaker had stolen the gift that Lord Marmoo promised to the spider queen? He paced, grinding his mouthparts, feeling his anger rise. Then he calmed himself with thoughts of tomorrow; after they invaded the Amphibilands, he'd kill *dozens* of frogs, hundreds.

As he imagined the upcoming bloodbath, the crowd parted in a clattering of legs to reveal a squad of red-banded scorpions: the toughest fighters and trackers in the army.

"Reporting for duty, sir," one of them said, saluting with her pincer.

"I captured a frog," Pigo told them. "Threw him in that cage there."

"Yes, sir," the red-banded squad leader said. "We saw him."

"Apparently, the lizards let a sandpaper frog guard him—and instead, he helped the prisoner escape."

"We saw *him*, too, sir."

Pigo narrowed his main eyes. "What does he look like? Big frog? Tough?"

"Not particularly, sir. Small and quite young."

The anger returned in a red haze. "Take your squad, and find him. Find both of them."

"Easily done, sir. They're green-bellied cowards; they must be running to the one place they think is safe—the Amphibilands. They're hopping home."

"Yes," Pigo said, his mouthparts shifting into a grin. "Of course. Catch them before they reach the Veil. Catch them and bring them to me."

# 26

TWENTY MINUTES AFTER THEY left the scorpion encampment, Gee stumbled in the dunes and fell to his knees. The brutal yellow sun was shining down on the frogs, heating the sand and burning their skin.

Darel dropped his spear and hefted Gee to his feet. "I got you, Gee."

"Sorry," Gee said. "I'm still weak from the cage."

"Well, look on the bright side."

"What's that?"

"You lost some of your baby fat."

"Ha-ha."

But he smiled, and they struggled onward. Yet after hopping into the scouring wind for another hour, Darel realized they couldn't outrun any pursuer. Once the scorps noticed Gee was gone and sent trackers after them, they were finished. No frog could beat a scorpion in the desert.

That didn't stop him, though. He struggled

through the blinding light and bruising heat, his toe pads slipping in the sand and Gee's weight numbing his shoulder.

"We'll be okay if they don't realize we're gone until tonight," he mumbled.

Gee didn't answer. Too exhausted to even lift his head, he simply staggered on, inner eyelids closed and nostrils slitted against the sand.

The scorching sun sank slowly in the sky. The endless dunes rose and fell and slowly smoothed into scrubland, with low thorny bushes and patches of rough weeds. When the hazy orange light of the setting sun touched the wavy hills, Darel and Gee collapsed. Maybe Gee tripped, maybe Darel stumbled—either way, they found themselves suddenly splayed in the dirt.

Unable to hop any farther, they crawled beside a spiny shrub, and Darel draped his mercenary's cloak over it, forming a makeshift tent to give them a little shelter.

Without even hiding their tracks, they fell into an exhausted sleep.

# 27

HE SPIDER QUEEN'S WARRIORS carried her into the encampment on a silken litter that shone like silvery clouds.

Marmoo scuttled alongside, hiding his disgust. He enjoyed a little elegance, but Jarrah was soft. She wouldn't last two minutes in a battle. A good thing he didn't *need* her in a battle. He needed her to destroy the Veil, and for that, she was perfect.

Afterward, he'd sink his stinger in her neck. But at the moment, she was of key importance. So he kept his opinion to himself as her servants brought her to the elaborate silken tent that now rose beside his pavilion.

She stepped nimbly from the platform and inspected her new quarters. "An adequate job," she observed. "I will be almost comfortable here."

"We won't inconvenience you for too long," Marmoo assured her. "After you tear down the Veil tomorrow, you can return to your castle."

"Not until the turtle king is dead."

"I'll deliver him to you, if you wish. We can't attack the Coves directly, because the mangrove swamp's in the way. But when he hears the Amphibilands has fallen, he'll venture into the open—and I'll be waiting. Happy to drag him to your castle for you."

"Perhaps. Or perhaps I will dispose of him here. We shall see."

"As you wish." Marmoo gestured with a pincer toward her silken tent. "Well, you must be tired after our journey . . ."

Queen Jarrah inclined her head. "I'll admit I'm in the mood for a snack."

"Pigo!" Marmoo barked. "Fetch the frog."

"I'm sorry, my lord," Pigo said, scuttling forward. "The lizards have managed to misplace the frog."

"The frog is gone?" Marmoo snapped.

"Yes, my lord. Apparently, a croaker from the Amphibilands masqueraded as a sandpaper frog and infiltrated the lizard camp."

Marmoo's mouthparts chewed angrily. "A *frog* did this?"

"A frog named Darel."

"A croaker?" Marmoo snarled. "A croaker snuck into my camp? He stole my prisoner, my gift to the queen?"

"Yes, my lord."

Marmoo's tail swayed dangerously above him. "Somebody must pay for this, Pigo."

Pigo bowed his head, standing still and silent.

With a sudden flick, Marmoo's stinger blurred toward Pigo—then stopped a fraction of an inch from his neck. "Find me that frog, commander. Bring him to me."

"I've sent the elite squad to catch him, my lord."

"Very good." Marmoo slitted his side eyes at Pigo. "*They* won't fail me."

"I'm sure you're right, Lord Marmoo," Jarrah said,

in her whispery voice. "However, I'm also disap-pointed. You promised me a taste of frog. Is *this* how you keep your word?"

Marmoo felt a cold rage rising inside him. To be embarrassed like this in front of a loathsome spider. He hated all frogs on principle—but for the first time in a long time, he had reason to hate one personally. When the red-banded squad returned, he would make this Darel pay dearly.

"I thought, my lord," Pigo said, his voice deeply respectful, "that by way of apology we might offer the queen her choice of . . . morsels."

Marmoo watched as Pigo's men shoved five strug-gling lizards toward the queen—including the lizard captain; Nogo, the rock lizard; and the three-toed skink.

"I like the way you think, Pigo," Marmoo said. "The lizards made the error, so let them pay for it. If that will suit you, Queen Jarrah?"

She prowled along the line of lizards, stroking the one-eyed captain's cheek, then squeezing the skink's arm with her long fingers, as if she were checking fruit for ripeness. The skink twitched with panic, and she slowed down, clearly enjoying his fear.

"So tomorrow morning . . ." Jarrah swiped a long, fuzzy leg across the rock lizard's chest. "You will escort me to the Outback Hills, Lord Marmoo?"

"Indeed, Queen Jarrah. In fact—" He turned to Pigo. "Position the army tonight. Surround the Amphibilands as completely as possible with the Veil still in place. We will not let a single frog escape."

"Yes, my lord."

A terrified squeal sounded from the three-toed skink as the spider queen began draping him in her webbing.

"If you'll excuse me, Queen Jarrah," Marmoo said. "I should oversee the placement of the troops."

"Of course, Lord Marmoo," she said, licking her fangs.

He spun on his mid-legs and crossed to the command tent. He consulted the maps, issuing orders and barking commands until the elite squad of red-banded soldiers returned.

"Where are the escaped frogs?" he asked them.

"They have vanished, my lord," the leader said. "We found no trace of them between here and the Amphibilands."

"You lost them."

"I beg your pardon, my lord, but either they sprouted wings or—"

Marmoo lowered his stinger until the sharp point hovered an inch from the squad leader's face. "Or what?"

"Or they headed in the opposite direction."

"Away from their home? They're pathetic little frogs, you fool. They'd never brave the outback. You must've lost them."

"Yes, my lord. I take full responsibility for our failure."

"Good," Marmoo said, and stung her.

The body collapsed, and the other red-banded scorpions shifted uneasily. They didn't like not having someone to obey.

"You," Marmoo said, pointing at another member of the squad. "You're the leader now."

# 28

N THE MOONLIGHT, COORAH FOLLOWED the trail toward the first peak of the Outback Hills.

She'd been camping in the hills for days, digging ditches and building barricades to slow the inevitable scorpion invasion. Well, that and healing injuries.

With all the earthmoving and tree felling, a half dozen frogs had been hurt before they ever saw a scorpion warrior. Plus, she and her father had had to work through the night to save the two injured frogs who'd survived the attempt to warn the turtle king.

She'd never seen such wounds before. The cuts and slashes were bad enough, but the scorpion poison made the injuries ten times worse.

Her father had cleaned a puncture wound on the unconscious bullfrog's shoulder, then just stopped.

"What's wrong?" Coorah had asked him.

"I can't stitch the wound closed," he said. "Not while there's still scorpion venom inside the cut."

"I think—" Coorah inflated her throat. "I think we need to draw the poison out."

"How?"

"With an infusion of billygoat plum tree."

He eyed her dubiously. "Are you sure?"

"That's what Grandmother's books say."

"But we don't *have* an infusion like that."

"Actually, Dad, um . . ." Coorah took a little earthen jar from a shelf, one of the many concoctions she'd prepared but never used. "It's right here."

She'd poured the medicine on the wound, and the bullfrog had groaned in pain. But a short time later the poison bubbled out of the wound. When they dabbed it away, the cut looked clean and healthy, and Coorah's father was able to stitch it closed.

"I was wrong about your studies," he'd said when he finished. "Your grandmother told you to follow your heart—and she was right. Your heart just saved a life."

And now, as she climbed into the moonlit hills, he was frantically reading the old books himself, trying to learn a little about battlefield medicine before the attack.

When she reached the top of the trail, Coorah sighed and patted her pouch of bandages and healing herbs. She'd finally had the chance to test her new medicines, and she wished she hadn't. Still, she knew she'd see far worse before this was over.

"Can't sleep?" Arabanoo asked, hopping into step beside her.

"I need more lemon-bark leaves. And"—she gave a weak croak—"I'll sleep when this is over."

"Yeah." He snapped a twig from a bush. "I keep thinking about Darel and Gee . . ."

"You don't even *like* them."

"Maybe not," Arabanoo said. "But they're the only frogs in the Amphibilands who aren't boring."

"The *only* frogs?" she asked. "What about me? I'm *fascinating*."

Arabanoo kicked a dirt clod. "Well, other than you."

"I'm also modest," she informed him.

He flicked his inner eyelids. "And apparently bull-headed. I heard your father say you weren't allowed to be up here alone."

"He says it's too dangerous." She glanced at the white-lipped tree frog. "Just like your mom told you."

"She says we're too young. Like the *scorpions* will care about that."

Coorah nodded. "Yeah. And I think about Darel and Gee, out there somewhere. They're our age and . . . well, I hope they're okay."

"Darel's too stubborn to die," Arabanoo said, "and Gee's too hungry."

She almost smiled. "You'd like each other if you ever—"

An alarm whistle cut through the night.

"Scorpions in the hills!" Arabanoo gasped, and sprang toward the sound.

Coorah started to follow. Then she remembered the drills and hopped back down the slope. She had to make sure other frogs had heard the alarm. At the bottom of the hill, on the edge of the eucalyptus forest, dozens of frogs stood at the makeshift barricades and in the tunnels and pits. In the branches above, half-hidden tree frogs crouched beside piles of rocks and eyed the gloom. They had heard the alarm and were alert and waiting.

In the quiet of the evening, a shout echoed from the hills—then the scuffle of fighting, and a scream.

Coorah grabbed her supplies and hopped back toward the fighting: She needed to be close in case anyone required treatment. By the time she reached the ridge, though, the clamor of battle from the second hill had ceased.

In the pale moonlight, she crept toward the hilltop, trying to find the source of a faint moaning. There was no sign of scorpions, but a dozen frogs lay in dark humps on the ground.

As she moved to help a wounded warrior, Arabanoo stepped from the cover of the thick brush. "They're gone," he told her, as he helped apply a poultice.

"Who were they?" she asked.

"Scouts. A few scouts. We got completely slammed by a few scorps, Coorah. There's no way we're going to win when the whole army attacks."

# 29

AREL WOKE IN THE DARK WITH A jerk. Where was he? What was that *noise*?

Sounded like a beast charging at him. An angry beast with small red eyes and big curving tusks. He reached for his dagger but instead touched something soft and warm—and realized that the grunting beast was just Gee snoring.

He smiled and blinked a few times. In the first faint light of the Australian dawn, he checked his surroundings: He was hunched in a makeshift tent in the middle of nowhere.

Except not really the middle of nowhere. They were at least halfway to the Turtle Coves.

Before leaving the scorpion encampment the previous day, Gee had clung to a tent peg with his toe pads and refused to budge. "We're going to warn the turtle king," he'd said. "That's final."

"You're too weak," Darel told him again, though he'd longed to see the Coves and warn the king. "You might not make it."

"Sometimes you need to make hard choices, Darel," Gee said, his voice soft but determined. "This isn't just sticking up for me with Arabanoo. The entire Amphibilands is at stake."

Darel had realized that Gee was right—and was braver than he'd ever known. They needed to warn the turtle king—even if it meant death for them both.

His mind still fogged with sleep, Darel peered uneasily at the sky. How long had they slept? Were they too late already?

"Gee!" he said, nudging his friend. "Wake up."

"What? Where?" Gee woke with a snort, then yawned hugely. "What are we doing in—" His eyes bulged as he remembered. "Oh! The turtles."

"Yeah. How're you feeling?"

"Good. Better." He thought for a second. "Hungry."

Darel handed him a bag of dried beetles.

"Eww," Gee said, after tasting a couple. "What're these?"

"Scorpion food."

"No wonder scorpions are so cranky." Gee tossed

a beetle in the air and caught it with his tongue. "If they ate honey snails, maybe they'd stop trying to kill everyone all the time."

Darel stretched. "You can suggest that to the turtle king when we meet him. We'll throw snails at the scorps."

"*Honey* snails," Gee corrected. "Regular snails wouldn't work. But first we've got to find the turtles. Can we get there in time?"

"I don't know," Darel said, chewing a beetle as he hopped out of the tent. "We've got to try."

"Yeah." Gee hopped out beside him. "And when we reach the Coves, everything's going to be pill-bug custard and cherry pie. I heard that the streets are paved with—"

"Swamp," Darel said, peering into the distance.

"Paved with *swamp*?" Gee croaked. "No, paved with—"

"Swamp," Darel repeated, pointing.

There, just ahead, the scrubland turned to mangrove swamp. First, the low shrubs grew taller, and then, *boom*, they exploded into dense green giants. And an instant after Darel saw the swamp, he smelled it: a briny, moist, muddy scent.

"Whoa," Gee gasped. "The Coves are on the other side of *that*?"

"Yeah, on the coast."

"I guess that's why the scorps don't invade. There's no way they could march through that."

"Not with all the sea snakes and crocodiles that live in there. They'd eat the scorps alive."

"In that case," Gee said, "it's good to be a frog! At least we can swim!" He bounded toward the mangrove swamp with Darel fast on his heels.

They scampered from the hardscrabble hills into a maze of green bushes at the outskirts of the swamp. The morning breeze carried the scent of salt water as they shoved through the bushes, then stopped at the bank of a wide, slow-moving saltwater river.

Mangrove trees towered on the far bank, with drooping branches and looping roots that arched above the water before disappearing below the brackish surface.

"On second thought," Gee said, "I'd rather be a bird. We've got to go *through* that?"

"Yeah—and fast."

With the sun rising behind him, Darel waded into the river, his hand on his dagger. Despite the calming, salty coolness seeping through his skin, he kept his eyes alert for any sign of danger.

"Cannonball!" Gee croaked, and splashed into the water beside him.

So much for stealth.

They swam across the river with powerful frog-strokes, then hauled themselves into the roots of a mangrove tree and wiped the water from their faces.

They slipped from the roots of that tree to the next one, following the path of a narrow waterway, a curving river inside the swamp.

As the dawn grew brighter, the overhanging leaves were reflected in the rippling river, and the water looked like a fat green snake. Strange noises sounded in the distance: the call of a bird Darel didn't recognize, and a moist, sucking sound.

At a sudden splash, Darel and Gee froze. A moment later, a swirl of water moved past them. Darel peered into the depths but couldn't tell if he'd really seen scales and claws and teeth or just imagined them.

But a few minutes later, as they followed a river bend, he knew he wasn't imagining the slitted reptilian eyes watching them from the water.

"Hey, Darel," Gee whispered. "You see him?"

"I see *them*," he answered, and gestured to the two other sets of eyes.

Gee bit his lower lip. "Maybe these are *friendly* crocs."

A spout of water erupted at them, and a massive pair of jaws lunged forward. Teeth glistened and mud splattered as the crocodile came right at the frogs.

Gee jumped straight up—faster than Darel had ever seen him move—and grabbed a thick, vine-draped branch with his finger pads. Darel swiped his dagger at the croc, but the beast kept coming, his close-set eyes glittering with malice.

Darel tensed to leap away but was afraid that the moment he was in the air the croc would snap his jaws closed around him.

"Hey!" Gee croaked. "Scaly-butt!"

The croc roared and lifted his head, snapping at Gee's dangling legs.

Gee yelped and pulled himself higher in the man-grove tree—and Darel leaped onto the crocodile's ridged back, then flung himself into a neighboring tree.

He scrambled higher, breathing heavily. "I guess these aren't the friendly ones," he said once his breathing had returned to normal.

With Gee muttering that they weren't *tree* frogs, they hopped from branch to branch, staying high above the swirling swamp. The three crocodiles followed them below, lazily swishing their powerful tails through the water.

Darel and Gee wandered deeper into the swamp, until they finally lost the crocs, then followed the flow of the sluggish water toward the coast. Darel pushed himself faster as the sun rose higher in the sky. The scorpions were invading the Amphibilands today, and he and Gee hadn't even found the turtles yet.

Had the spider queen already destroyed the Veil? Were the scorpions swarming through the Outback Hills? Were they hunting frogs in the eucalyptus forest or closing in on the triplets in the nursery pools? And what about Coorah and his mom?

Without the Kulipari, they didn't have a chance.

In the distance, Darel heard the sound of surf. He opened his nostrils wide and sniffed. "What's that?"

"Sounds like waves," Gee said. "We're close."

"No, I mean the smell."

Gee closed his inner eyelids and inhaled. "That's you, Darel. You need to wash behind your ears."

"Not *me*! That's . . . that's freshwater."

"Weird." Gee sniffed again and nodded. "Coming from over there."

They started toward the smell. The sound of the surf grew louder as they followed the swampy river, and in the distance they saw where the trees stopped and the clear blue sky started.

"We did it!" Gee cried. "We reached the Coves!"

"I hope we're in time."

Darel bounded ahead, three quick leaps—and a huge crocodile mouth broke the surface of the water directly in front of him.

Gee croaked a warning, and Darel spun in the air and pulled his dagger, his blade no bigger than one of the croc's teeth.

*Too late.* The gaping jaws snapped around Darel.

# 30

HE CROCODILE'S TEETH CLOSED around Darel—very gently, like a mother cradling her tadpoles.

Gee bellowed a desperate war cry and slammed face-first into the croc's snout. Then he fell with a splat into the mud and groaned faintly.

"Oh!" a voice said. "Terribly sorry, I didn't mean to frighten you! Well, if you *are* frightened. Perhaps you're not. Perhaps that was a scream of glee—or a greeting! Perhaps that is how frogs say hello to crocodiles—headfirst."

Darel gingerly slipped from the crocodile's mouth and peered past the beast's huge head. There, on a saddle strapped to the croc's back, loosely holding reins, was a turtle. A youngish turtle, by the look of him, with a broad brown shell and an extremely long neck.

At the end of the long neck, a round face smiled at Darel—and kept talking.

"Now, turtles, being perhaps less creative than frogs, usually shake flippers in greeting. Or wave. Or say 'Hello' or 'How do you do?' If we're in a more formal setting, we might say 'Pleased to meet you' or 'The pleasure's all mine' or— Oh, are you stuck in the mud?" The long-necked turtle chortled. "No, no! We don't say *that*, not in formal settings! I mean you down there, frog in the mud. Do you require assistance?"

Darel glanced at Gee and saw him standing knee-deep in the muck.

"Um," Gee said, his eyes bulging nervously as he considered the crocodile.

Darel hopped to the riverbank. "We *could* use some assistance, yes," he told the long-necked turtle. "We're looking for Sergu—the king of the turtles."

"Oh, thank goodness! I was afraid you were going to ask for assistance with—I don't know—ribbeting or hopping or some such. I mean to say, with *frog*like behavior, and I wouldn't have been any help at all. But if you're seeking Sergu, well! Well, well, well!"

"Um," Darel said. "Well?"

"Well, climb aboard!" The turtle beamed, patting his crocodile mount. "And I'll take you to him!"

"You know King Sergu?"

"Know him? I am his apprentice! Well, one of his

apprentices, though I'm his star pupil, if I do say so myself. Which I often do. Say so myself, I mean." The turtle suddenly gasped. "Oh! Pardon me! Terrible manners, not introducing myself. My name is Yarban, but they call me Yabber. Some people think"—the turtle lowered his voice confidingly—"that I talk too much."

"That's ridiculous," Darel said, suppressing a grin as he scrambled onto the croc.

"Is your friend coming?" Yabber asked.

"C'mon, Gee."

Gee puffed out his throat and didn't budge. "Do you honestly think I'm going to ride a croc?"

"A minute ago you were going to attack him. C'mon, we're running out of time."

"The only reason *you're* not scared of the croc," Gee grumbled, "is because you know it'd eat *me* first."

Darel grinned and helped Gee onto the croc's back. Then he said, "I'm Darel. This is Gee. We're from the Amphibilands."

"Very pleased to meet you!" the turtle cried, turning the crocodile toward the Coves. "Never met a frog from the Amphibilands before, but I can already tell I'm going to like you."

Darel grabbed on to the saddle as the crocodile

surged forward. It followed the brackish waterways until they emerged from the swamp. After the crowded darkness of the mangrove trees, the world seemed suddenly bright and open, and Darel shot his tongue at a passing fly for a celebratory snack.

"Now, shall I give you the tour?" Yabber asked. "To your left, you can see the freshwater lagoon; that's where we long-neck turtles live."

"That's why we smelled freshwater," Darel said.

"Ahead and to your right," Yabber continued, "past the beach, is the ocean where the flatback turtles—such as our good king—live, in those lovely homes among the grassy shallows and, of course, in the coral reef. They are sea turtles."

In Darel's daydreams, he'd imagined the Coves as a grand and ornate city, but in reality it looked simple and comfortable. Turtles lolled around the freshwater lagoon, some basking in the morning light, while sea turtles swam in the ocean shallows between half-submerged homes built of long, swaying grasses and colorful coral.

". . . pleased to invite you to a dinner of sea cucumber and striped shrimp," Yabber was saying. "King Sergu is particularly fond of crabs—though I prefer worms myself, having a more delicate constitution. How does that sound? A feast, to welcome you as guests. And of course for dessert—"

"Yabber!" Darel interrupted. "This is an emergency. We're here because we're in trouble—the Amphibilands is in trouble. We need the king's help."

Yabber cocked his round head. "Oh, my goodness. Help with what?"

"Well, do you know about the Veil?"

"Do I know about the Veil? What I don't know about the Veil, my long-toed friend, would fit inside a prawn's nostril! I'm the king's star pupil, after all—did I mention that?—and the second-most-powerful dreamcaster in the Coves!" Yabber looped his long neck toward Darel. "Of course, saying that I'm the second-most-powerful dreamcaster is like saying that in a race between a slug and a hawk, the slug is the second fastest! Or in a fight between a crocodile and a possum, the possum is the second fiercest. Or in a—"

"We get the idea!" Darel interrupted, a little desperately. "Now take us to the king, please—as fast as you can."

"And that's just *dream*casters," Yabber said, turning his croc toward the beach. "The spider queen is more powerful than me—than I? I think 'than I.' Is it *me* or *I*? She's more powerful, but she's a *night*caster, and of course nightcasting is a warped, evil offshoot of dreamcasting . . ."

Yabber babbled on. Darel only halfway listened to the turtle as they moved away from the lagoon and onto the beach. He watched as shallow waves in the protected bay washed through the sea turtle city, turned waterwheels, gently lifted unmoored buildings, and then receded.

Sea turtles swam with gliding strokes through the blue water, some busy at a sea cucumber farm, others ducking through coral arches. Young turtles lazed on the beach or waddled along sandy paths and slipped into the surf. Hatchlings dug through huge heaps of sand, building elaborate castles and forts.

Finally, Yabber brought his croc to a halt near a noisy bunch of hatchlings clambering all over an old turtle lying on his side in the sand. The little turtles were climbing high on the old fellow's tilted shell, then sliding down.

As the hatchlings shouted with glee, Yabber said, "May I introduce you to His Glorious Majesty, the wisest reptile to ever wear a shell—King Sergu!"

Darel looked around. "Um. Where?"

# 31

IGHT THERE." YABBER SLID from his croc to the beach. "I told him to expect you—I sent a message via dreamcasting, you know. I am the second-most-powerful dreamcaster in the Coves, after all. Perhaps I mentioned that?"

"Yes!" Gee said, hopping down beside him. "We know, we know. Star pupil. Um, did you say something about grilled shrimp?"

"Do you like honey-glazed? I've got caramelized worms in the saddlebag, too. I'll just—"

"Um, where's the king again?" Darel asked.

"Here," a deep voice said.

The old turtle whose shell the hatchlings were using as a slide raised his head and inspected Darel and Gee with gentle golden eyes.

*That* was the king? Darel had expected a grand and powerful ruler on a shining throne, not a sleepy old turtle dozing on the beach.

"Oh!" Darel said, with an awkward bow. "Oh, Your, um, Majesty. Hello, I, um, didn't know that was you."

"Well, of course you didn't," King Sergu said, solemnly. "We've never met. I'm sure I'd remember such a fine pair of wood frogs."

"Yes, sir—erm, Your Majesty."

"I recognize that dagger on your hip, though," the turtle king told Darel.

"You do? It was my father's."

The king's golden eyes brightened, and a smile creased his leathery face. "You are Apari's son?"

"Yes! How did you—" Darel's eyes bulged. "Wow. You knew my father?"

"He was a great frog and a good friend." The king raised a flipper and touched Darel's shoulder. "It was your father who saved my life in the war."

"I—I didn't know," Darel said, a little stunned.

"Well, your mother is not one to brag. But

why are you so far from home? Come closer and tell me what brings you to the Coves."

Darel gathered his thoughts. "Well, Your Majesty . . . the Amphibilands is under attack. Gee and I saw a scorpion patrol in the Outback Hills, inside your Veil." He told the whole story as Gee downed a dozen shrimp. He ended with ". . . and now the spider queen is destroying the rest of the Veil while Lord Marmoo's scorpion army prepares to invade."

Silence fell, except for the sound of the surf and distant shouts of hatchlings.

The king doodled in the sand with a flipper for what felt like a long time. Then he looked at Darel and frowned. "You are correct—the Amphibilands is in grave danger. Even as we speak, the spider queen is unraveling the Veil."

"Right *now*?" Darel asked, his nostrils tightening in despair. "Are you sure? How do you know?"

"I was dreamcasting while you told your tale, Darel. Dreamcasting is a discipline of the mind; we do not require webs and poisons and chants."

"Oh."

"Now, hush." The king closed his eyes. "I must concentrate."

Then nothing happened.

The surf crashed. The hatchlings tumbled into a big hole they'd dug. A long-necked turtle trundled past with a coral cart.

And still, nothing happened.

Gee tossed a shrimp into the air, caught it with his tongue, then whispered to Yabber, "What's he doing?"

"Well, he's not practicing the backstroke," Yabber replied. "He's dreamcasting."

"*That's* dreamcasting? He just closes his eyes?"

"Not impressive enough for you?" Yabber waggled his scaly eyebrows. "You'd prefer that the king dance around a bonfire while twenty-seven sandpipers beat upon his shell? 'Just closes his eyes?' *You* try it, longlegs!"

"I would," Gee muttered, "but I'd probably fall asleep."

Darel stretched out on the beach as the sun warmed the morning, his mind miles away. Instead of seeing the crystal water, he saw the huge scorpion encampment, the rows of brutal troops with poisonous stingers. He also saw the Amphibilands, the tadpool nursery and marketplace. He heard the peaceful burble of water and the chirp of tree frogs. He saw his mother sitting in her shop, chatting with a customer as she arranged a bouquet.

Finally, King Sergu opened his eyes. "I'm too late."

# 32

N THE PEAK OF THE OUTBACK HILL
nearest the desert, Pigo watched
as Queen Jarrah wove a spiky web
between a boulder and the branches
of a crooked tree. The strands glistened with droplets of poison in the morning sun.

"Some spiders weave orbs," the queen told Lord
Marmoo, as she spun. "Some weave funnels. Others
spin tubes or domes."

"And what is *that*?" he asked, bending his forelegs
for a closer look.

"A tangle web. See how messy, how chaotic?
But every strand has purpose and power. This, Lord
Marmoo, is the web that will crush the Veil."

As she spun arcane patterns into the web, her
ladies-in-waiting lofted strands of silk into the air,
thin lines that floated into the sky, arching over the
still-hidden Amphibilands until the glinting threads
disappeared from view.

The spider queen breathed on the tangle web, and

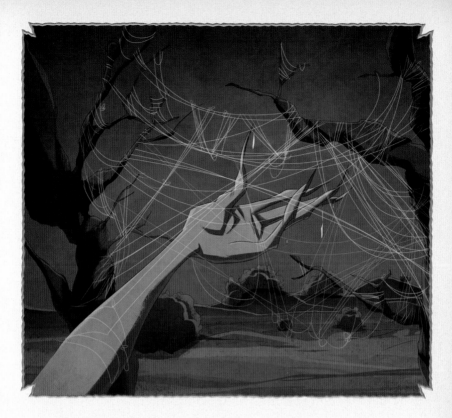

a loud whine sounded from the strands. A stench crept into the morning air while Jarrah crooned under her breath, stroking the web. In a circle around her, the ladies-in-waiting dropped venom onto the silk they were loosing into the sky.

Invisible *things* seemed to slither in the air. A few of Pigo's warriors clenched their pincers nervously, but he kept his face impassive even as Jarrah's power oozed around him.

Then an ear-piercing whine echoed over the hills, the sound of the nightcast web scraping at the Veil, and

Jarrah's chanting grew louder and madder, her hands a blur on her web, strumming smoky, nightmarish shapes from the poison silk, until suddenly—

Silence.

No sound, no wind, no stench. No earthquake of nightcast power.

And into the quiet, the queen spoke. "The turtle king is reaching out from the Coves, trying to stop me." Her triumphant laugh rang in the hills. "And he is failing. Oh, he slowed me a little, but soon I'll rip his Veil into shreds—"

With a whip crack of thunder, the whine started again, the ladies-in-waiting spooling silk into the sky and the queen spinning at a furious rate.

# 33

O N THE QUIET BEACH, THE TURTLE king sighed. "I've protected the frog nation for a hundred years. I've watched generations grow from tadpole to frog. The Amphibilands is my greatest achievement, a safe and unspoiled sanctuary."

"But—" Darel's eyes bulged. "But you're too late?"

King Sergu nodded sadly. "I can't stop Queen Jarrah, not from this far away."

"So they're going to invade," Darel said. A sick feeling rose in his gut. "They're really going to invade. You have to do something. My mom's there, and the triplets—"

"My whole family," Gee croaked, kicking the sand.

"And Coorah and the chief, and . . . *everyone*."

"We've got to get back." Gee looked toward the mangrove swamp. "Help them fight and—"

"No," Darel interrupted, puffing his throat in agitation. "What we need is the Kulipari."

"Indeed we do," the turtle king said.

"Where are they?"

"They're here. They've been in seclusion, Darel."

"They've been *training*," Yabber added, stretching his neck high. "With the king. He teaches 'em how to tap into their poison—that's the key. Now, you're both wood frogs, you don't have poison, but—"

"So they're still around?" Gee blurted. "The Kulipari?"

"Oh, yes, yes, yes!" Yabber nodded emphatically. "Most of the Kulipari didn't survive the Hidingwar, and those who did . . . well, they depleted their faculties."

"They what-ed their what-ulties?" Gee asked.

"They ran out of poison," Yabber explained, "and now they're ordinary frogs. There's a new generation, though. That's who His Cartilaginous Majesty has been training, a new generation of Kulipari that—"

"Where are they?" Darel said, hopping in impatience. "Have you called them? You need to call them. Where are they?"

"I'm not sure they're ready." The turtle king spoke slowly, his eyes thoughtful. "They've just finished training, and—"

"Not *ready*?" Darel interrupted. "The Amphibi-lands isn't ready, either. I wasn't ready; Gee wasn't ready. Ready or not, we need them. We need them now."

"You're right." King Sergu nodded. "The time has come for the Kulipari to fight again." He turned to Yabber. "Come along."

The turtles waddled into the surf, then shot grace-fully through the water toward the coral reef.

# 34

AREL GAZED EXCITEDLY ACROSS the bay to the broad coral avenue where the king and Yabber were rising from the water. He was finally going to meet the Kulipari! And they'd save the Amphibilands.

He watched as the two turtles climbed a spiraling tower to a conch shell poised on top. The king blew a series of notes.

"What's he doing?" Gee asked.

"Calling the Kulipari, I guess," Darel said, grinning happily. "Now we just have to wait. They'll handle the scorps. Pass me a snack."

"I don't know," Gurnugan

said, tossing a shrimp for Darel to catch with his tongue. "You think the Kulipari can handle all this? They almost went extinct last time, and the scorpions never joined with the spiders before."

"There are probably a hundred Kulipari by now, maybe two hundred!" Darel's eyes bulged at the thought of an army of elite warrior frogs. "Sure, they never faced a horde this big—but a hundred Kulipari can do *anything*."

They sat on the beach, eating from Yabber's stash of food until their stomachs bulged. A few turtle hatchlings came to stare, and Gee made them giggle by telling them he was a turtle who'd lost his shell and begging them to help him find it.

Finally, Yabber and the king returned to the beach.

"Are they coming?" Darel asked.

"They'll be here any moment," the king assured him.

Darel stood at attention. "Do I look okay?" he asked Gee.

Gee goggled at him. "*What?*"

"Nothing," Darel mumbled, his nostrils flared in embarrassment. "I just can't believe I'm going to meet the Kulipari."

Darel scanned the lagoon eagerly, anxious for

his first sight of the superpowered frogs. Were there a hundred of them? *Two* hundred? Would they accept him as a trainee? He'd happily sharpen the weapons and polish the shields. Well, at least at first.

And suddenly . . . there!

*Frogs.* A small squad of Kulipari approached from the direction of the swamp, probably the advance scouts, only four of them.

Still, Darel stared eagerly, memorizing every detail, puffing his throat in excitement.

The one in front looked fierce. He prowled closer, with the assurance of a predator. He was the second tallest of this squad, his skin glossy green, with orange and black markings. He wore a billowing cloak, and two big boomerangs were strapped in an *X* across his back.

"That's Burnu," Yabber said. "The squad leader. He's completely fearless, the most skilled fighter among them."

"And the most arrogant," the turtle king muttered.

Darel's wide-eyed gaze switched to the largest of the squad, a huge frog with broad shoulders and arms that rippled with muscle. He wore spiked bracers on his wrists and a bunch of pouches on his belt that reminded Darel of Coorah's.

"What's in that big guy's pouches?" Gee asked, apparently noticing the same thing.

"Herbs," the turtle king said. "That's Ponto. He's a healer."

"A healer?" Gee snorted. "Looks more like a *hurter.*"

"He's that, too, when necessary. He's as tough as a leatherback's shell and as strong as a tidal wave."

Darel hopped from one foot to the other, looking at a third member of the squad, a red-and-black frog with a longbow strapped across her chest and a quiver peeking over one shoulder. In a flash, she leaped ahead of the others. She somersaulted twice in the air, laughing at something Darel didn't hear.

He laughed, too—from the excitement of actually seeing them in person.

The Kulipari. They were everything he'd imagined, and more.

"That's Dingo," Yabber announced.

"Like the wild dog?" Gee asked.

"Don't let her hear you say that," Yabber told him. "Or she'll stick your toe pads to your forehead. She's the fastest one of them, like lightning on a deadline—and that's *before* she taps her poison."

"She must learn to curb her tongue," the king said. "And not treat everything like a joke."

"Dingo knows when to get serious," Yabber said.

"I hope so," the king grumbled.

"Who's the fourth one?" Darel asked in an awed whisper, staring at a green frog in a hooded cloak, carrying a tall, gnarled staff.

She moved gracefully, like a dancer—or a hunter. Her pretty face and slender build didn't disguise her strength.

"There are only three of them, Darel," Gee said, then immediately corrected himself. "Oh! I didn't notice her at first."

"Yes, she does that," Yabber said, with a chuckle. "Her name's Quoba. She's the second-in-command—and the scout."

"Pretty good at sneaking around, huh?"

"She could shave a nervous chipmunk before it knew she was there!" Yabber said. "Not that she ever *would*. I mean, what good is a bald chipmunk?"

Darel laughed and turned to Gee. "See? I told you! The scorps don't stand a chance." Then he looked back to Yabber, his eyes bulging. "Where are the rest of them?"

"The rest of whom?"

Darel hopped a few times in excitement. "Of the Kulipari! How many are there? A hundred? *Two* hundred?"

"Oh." For the first time since they'd met him, Yabber seemed speechless.

"This is all of them, Darel," the king said. "Only four Kulipari remain."

The world spun, and Darel felt suddenly light-headed. Only four? Only *four* Kulipari to fight Marmoo's endless horde and the spider queen's evil magic?

Dozens of Kulipari had died in the Hidingwar. How could *four* defeat an even stronger enemy?

"We're in big trouble," he said.

# 35

FTER TALKING WITH JARRAH, LORD Marmoo skittered over to Pigo, a hard glint in his malevolent eyes.

Pigo resisted the urge to shift uneasily at his lordship's expression. "Yes, my lord?"

"I am running out of patience with that eight-legged freak," Marmoo said, his mouthparts moving into a snarl.

"Is the turtle king slowing her down?"

"So she claims," Marmoo said. "Though she also claims she'll finish ripping the Veil to shreds before the sun sets."

"You don't believe her?"

"Oh, I believe her." Marmoo snapped one of his claws closed. "She wouldn't dare lie to me. But I refuse to wait for sunset. At least here in this corner of the Outback Hills, the turtle king's magic is completely crushed. Look around, Pigo."

Pigo obediently surveyed the craggy hilltop with his main eyes while glancing with his side eyes at the ravine with green leaves, which led deeper into the hills, closer to the heart of the Amphibilands.

"You're looking at an open door," Marmoo told him. "There's no reason to wait for the Veil to fall completely—we'll pour through these hills in killing waves."

"Yes, my lord. However, the army is positioned in a wide circle around—"

"So reposition them!" Marmoo's tail whipped in the air.

Pigo stared in surprise. Most scorpions couldn't change their minds as easily as that. Once they made a plan, they stuck to it even if the circumstances changed. But then, Lord Marmoo wasn't like most scorpions.

"We'll attack from a single point instead of surrounding the frogs," Marmoo continued, his scarred face alight. "Instead of invading this evening, we'll invade in a matter of hours . . . And tonight, little brother, we'll feast."

## 36

AREL KEPT CATCHING HIMSELF gazing at the Kulipari—first at the leader, Burnu, and then at the others. Maybe there were only four of them, but they seemed to glow with strength.

He remembered his father looking that way back when he was a tadpole. Maybe this was his big chance, the one he'd been dreaming of all his life—a way to join the Kulipari. There were only four of them, so they'd need all the help they could get.

Meanwhile, King Sergu and Yabber briefed the Kulipari. Well, mostly Yabber briefed them, finishing with ". . . and His Majestic Turtleness did a little dreamcasting and discovered that Queen Jarrah has already ripped a hole in the Veil."

"The scorpions are invading?" Burnu said. "Then what're we waiting for?"

Gee looked up. "A plan? A sign? A stroke of luck? Reinforcements?"

"We don't need any of that," Burnu replied, with a cocky flick of his inner eyelids. "The four of us can defeat *any* army. We'll—"

"My dad!" Darel suddenly blurted.

Everyone stopped and looked at him. "Yes, Darel?" Quoba asked. "Your father?"

The words came in an excited jumble. "He was a Kulipari. He was a unit leader—so was my grandfather—and I've been training for this my whole life."

"Training for what?" Yabber asked.

"Nobody knows the Amphibilands like I do, every village and stream and—and . . ." Darel gulped hard. "I want to join. The Kulipari. I'll do whatever it takes. I'll work harder than—"

"Will you learn to tap your poison?" Burnu demanded, his brow cocked.

"Well, no," Darel said. "I don't have poison."

"Of course not. You're a mud frog."

"A *wood* frog," Gee said, sharply.

Burnu waved a hand dismissively. "Mud, dirt—whatever." He inspected Darel. "You don't have poison, so you don't have what it takes."

Darel's face felt hot, and he looked at his feet and wanted to disappear.

"Have *you* ever fought a scorpion?" Gee asked Burnu.

"No, but when I do, I'll *win*." He glanced disdainfully at Darel. "Not like your friend Muddy over there."

Dingo, who was walking on her hands in circles around the king, told Gee, "Burnu *did* pick a fight with a cricket once. He thought it called him a chirp."

Ponto hopped in front of her, and she bounced off him like she'd hit a boulder. "Pay attention," he rumbled.

"I was paying attention." She rubbed her butt, then muttered, "Burnu's not the only one who acts like a chirp."

"A 'chirp'?" Gee mouthed to Darel.

"I think she means 'jerk,'" he whispered miserably back. "Or 'chump.' Or something."

Burnu rolled his eyes. "Listen, we're not wood frogs. We're Kulipari—there's poison running through our veins. Any one of us could beat a *hundred* scorpions."

"That would be more reassuring," the king said, "if you were fighting four hundred scorpions. However, you're fighting thousands—and spiders, too."

"Spiders?" Ponto asked. "Spiders don't fight alongside scorps—they fight *against* scorps."

"They used to," the king said. "But this new scorpion lord has formed an alliance with the spider queen, my old student, Jarrah, who corrupted my teachings. She is a treacherous enemy."

"We can take her," Burnu said. "We can take all of them."

"We must beware," Quoba said, in her quiet voice, "of exhausting our power."

Burnu patted one of his boomerangs. "We're ready for this."

"Ready and eager!" Dingo said, her tongue shooting out to catch a passing blowfly. "Let's go kick some carapace."

Ponto cracked his knuckles. "That's right. There's only one thing scorps understand—force."

"But there's more than one way to beat them," Quoba said. "Look at Darel."

"At Muddy?" Burnu said. "Why?"

"Because he walked into the scorpion encampment with nothing but a dagger and his courage. Being brave when you're strong is easy; the real test comes when you're weak."

"Great, now I'm *weak* . . . ," Darel muttered.

"I'm simply saying," Quoba continued, "that perhaps there is a better way to proceed than rushing into battle."

"A better way than winning *quickly*?" Dingo asked. "You want to stretch this out like an emu's neck?"

Burnu snorted. "The scorpions are invading while we're twiddling our toe pads. The only question is, how do we get there in time?"

"You ride sailfish," the king announced, and he gestured with a flipper toward the water.

Four turtles stood in the rippling surf, each one holding the reins of a harnessed sailfish—long purple-and-silver fish with sword-like bills and high, ridged sails.

"Whoa," Gee said, gulping loudly. "We're going to *ride* those?"

"Indeed," the king said. "Down the coast, through the salt marsh, right into the heart of the eucalyptus forest in the Amphibilands."

"We're *frogs*," Gee said. "We don't last long in salt water."

"You won't be in the ocean," the king reassured him. "You'll be on it. And that's the quickest way. Yabber and I will follow on our crocodile mounts— which will be a trifle slower, I'm afraid."

"You're coming?" Darel asked.

"Of course," the old king said. "Once I arrive, I will try to protect the Veil."

"Sailfish!" Burnu exclaimed, grinning toward the water. "Perfect."

Darel swallowed and said, "I don't think a frontal attack is the best idea."

"Sure, Muddy," Burnu said. "Like you've got a better plan."

"Well . . ."

"Do I tell *you* how to look like a dirty puddle?"

"Um, no."

"So why are you telling *me* how to fight?" The Kulipari leader shook his head. "Everyone, fall in! We ride to war!"

Ponto swung his bulk onto a fish beside Burnu's, and Dingo did a backflip and landed on a fish on the squad leader's other side.

However, Quoba quietly turned to Darel. "You have an alternative plan?"

"Not exactly a *plan* . . ."

"What, then?"

"More of a vague idea."

"Tell us what you're thinking, Darel."

"Well . . ." Darel looked at old Sergu. "How much money does a king have?"

# 37

A T THE LOWER BARRICADES IN THE Outback Hills, Coorah watched Chief Olba speak to the hastily assembled militia. "We must stop the scorpion attack in the hills," she croaked. "If they reach the eucalyptus forest, the Amphibilands will fall."

An uneasy murmur spread through the crowd.

"They will tear down our homes and destroy our farms. They will show no mercy to elderly frogs or tadpoles. We *must* stop them in the hills." Olba drew herself up as tall as possible. "And we will! We fight together to defend our home!"

A smattering of shouts and stomps greeted Olba's words, but nobody sounded convinced. Coorah knew that none of the frogs expected to win this battle—they simply didn't have any choice but to fight it.

She turned to Arabanoo. "You're heading to the front?"

"Yeah," he said. "I heard the scorpions are massing

for the attack. I've got to leave before my mom stops me."

"Same with me and my dad," she said, patting her pouches. "So let's go."

"You should stay here, Coorah. You're going into battle with a bunch of herbs!"

"Who else is there?" She turned toward the hills. "My father's great at treating diseases, not war wounds. I've been praying for the Kulipari to come, but it looks like we're on our own. I'm needed there, to patch the wounded."

He sighed. "Just . . . be careful."

"I promise I'll look both ways before crossing the battlefield."

"Very funny."

They climbed the path toward the peak of the middle hill, where they intended to meet the invaders. Then they said good-bye, as Arabanoo continued onward and Coorah climbed a lookout tree to survey the battle and respond to any injuries.

As the midday sun shone above her, she watched frogs assemble at barricades and cluster in the tree-tops behind branches woven together for camouflage and protection.

They couldn't beat the scorpions in open battle,

strength against strength. They needed to use the land that they knew so well, setting traps and preparing sneak attacks. If tree frogs fought from the high branches and the burrowers from underground and the wood frogs from concealment, maybe they stood a chance.

A slim chance, but a chance.

On the next hill, Coorah suddenly saw scuttling black shapes. Scorpions. The way they moved set her nerves on edge: Too many legs, and those swaying tails looked like angry snakes, coiled to strike.

Then she realized they weren't *all* scorpions. A few platoons of spiders crawled along the edges of a granite outcropping, with bristly fur and white fangs, weaving silken throwing-nets.

Compared to them, the regiment of ferocious lizard mercenaries looked almost normal. They were at the front of the scorpion army, a solid mass of dull scales and lashing tails and ripping claws. Two huge rock lizards hefted a battering ram, and the mercenary soldiers all hissed in anticipation.

Coorah exhaled softly, then checked her pouches for the hundredth time that day. Everything in place. Now all she needed was for someone to get hurt.

What a cheerful thought.

She glanced toward the burrowing frogs peeking from their tunnels—and without a hint of warning, the enemy attacked.

A wedge of green and brown suddenly drove forward from the next hill, with shields clanking and claws slashing. The lizards. Hundreds of reptilian mouths roared a battle cry that shook the Outback Hills. Sharp teeth glinted, and forked tongues flicked.

Coorah saw a ripple of hesitation pass through the ranks of the frogs—they were fisherfolk and weavers, not warriors—then one brave frog croaked a battle cry at the advancing lizards, and the rest joined her.

The earth rumbled, rocks and battle nets filled the air . . . and the two armies met with a crash.

# 38

HE WAVES ROSE AND FELL AROUND Darel, and the wind cooled his face. He tasted the salt from the water through his skin. His purple fish shimmered in the sunlight, and a beautiful mosaic of colors wavered under the clear water like a field of wildflowers. A coral reef extended endlessly beneath them, with deep green stalks, bright yellow blossoms, and delicate blue spheres.

"Coorah would love this!" Darel called to Gee.

"She'd want to make coral medicine." Gee pointed out to sea and asked, "What's that?"

"A manta ray," Quoba told him. "Watch how she moves."

The manta seemed to glide through the currents, and Darel watched with bulging eyes, so amazed by the sights that he almost forgot his urgency.

Then Burnu croaked, "Hey, Muddy! Did you really walk into the scorpions' camp unarmed?"

Darel shrugged. "Well, I had my dagger."

"That's *crazy*," Dingo called, as her fish leaped over the one that carried Burnu and the two young frogs. "I mean, that's seriously insane."

She sounded pretty impressed, so Darel said, "Thanks."

"How'd a wood frog get that brave?" Ponto asked.

"Well, my dad was a Kulipari." Darel thought for a second. "And my mom's a wood frog. We never give up."

Burno trailed his finger pads in the water. "Your dad was a unit leader? What was his name?"

"Apari."

Burnu almost fell off their fish. "No way! Really?"

"Yeah. Why?"

"Did you hear that?" Burnu called to Quoba. "Darel is *Apari*'s son."

A sudden flame of hope ignited in Darel's chest. "Do you . . . do you know him?"

"What?" Burnu shook his head. "No. We've heard about him, though."

"Oh. For a second, I thought . . ." Darel gulped in disappointment. "I mean, everyone says he died, but they never found his body."

"You don't know the story?" Ponto asked.

"What story?"

Ponto shifted uncomfortably and didn't answer. Nobody said anything for a second, then Quoba's sailfish shot forward from behind and joined theirs.

"In the last battle," she told Darel, "your father saved King Sergu's life. The Kulipari were exhausted—all their poison burned out—but the scorps were still attacking. The king says he didn't have a chance."

"But he did. He survived."

"Because of your father."

"What did he do?"

"He'd used all his poison already. He was finished, empty." Quoba fell silent, and for a moment the only sound was the splashing of the fish. "Yet he managed to reach deep inside and find more power."

"Nobody knows how," Burnu said.

Quoba nodded. "Not even the turtle king. But your father did it. They say he glowed with power, as bright as the sun. He beat back the final scorpion attack, and then . . ."

"He died?" Darel asked, in a small voice.

She nodded.

"But they never found the body."

"There was no body," Burnu told him, sounding gentle for once. "Sergu says your father tapped so much power, and burned so brightly, that nothing was left but ash."

"Except the king was left," Quoba corrected. "And the Amphibilands was protected. And thousands of frogs lived safe from harm."

Sea spray misted Darel's face and felt like tears. He blinked his inner eyelids, then swallowed a few times. His father really was dead; the turtle king had seen him die.

Darel watched the coastline become greener and lusher as they approached the Amphibilands, and when he turned, Gee was right beside him.

"You okay?" Gee asked, after a while.

"Yeah," Darel said. "I guess I already knew he was dead. I just . . . wanted to see him again."

Gee nodded. "He was a real hero."

"Yeah."

"Stubborn, too," Gee said, as the sailfish veered into the salt marsh. "He didn't care that he was out of poison—he tapped it anyway."

That almost made Darel smile. "I wonder how he did it."

"You rescued me from the middle of the scorpion army, Darel. How'd you do *that*?"

"I didn't have any other choice."

# 39

OORAH WATCHED AS THE INVADING army of lizards leaped rows of sharpened logs and landed hip-deep in concealed patches of mud.

Swamp frogs released clouds of white fluffy "cotton" they'd gathered from bulrushes, which floated in the air and blocked the invaders' vision.

Half-blind lizards crashed into pits excavated by burrowing frogs. They stampeded forward and were tripped by the flicking tongues of wood frogs hiding in the leaves. The off-balance lizards slid down a mud chute into a pool, where water frogs tied them with thick vines.

Except that a dozen of the biggest lizards broke through and smashed a battering ram into the central barricade. The barricade shuddered but held.

Wounded frogs cried for help, and Coorah couldn't watch any longer. She raced into the fray.

Webs and nets twirled overhead, and a spear stabbed the ground a foot away, but she ignored all that. She crouched beside an injured frog to bind a cut, then wrapped another frog's leg.

While she was treating a head wound, a massive lizard loomed beside her. His tail pounded the ground, and he charged—but Coorah was prepared.

She reached into a pouch and tossed blue lily powder at the lizard's face. He roared, clawed at his eyes, and disappeared in the whirl of battle.

Coorah turned back to her patients, a blur of bandages and wounds. She used all her training. She'd always worried that she was being selfish, wasting time on something that didn't matter. Now she was saving lives.

Still, there were too many lizards driving forward, not to mention the scorpions and spiders massed behind them. She couldn't keep up with the injuries.

Across the battlefield, Arabanoo and his gang lured charging lizards into a trap of sticky sundew drops, where they stuck like flies. Wood frog hunters cut vines tying the tops of a dozen saplings to the ground; when the saplings sprang upward, they hurled vats of quick-hardening mud into the invading army.

Then waves of scorpions and spiders pushed past the lizards. Pincers snapped, tails lashed, and webs darkened the sky.

The frog defenders fell back, then fell back again, until finally, an urgent whistle cut through the clamor: Chief Olba sounding the retreat.

The frog army abandoned the middle hill.

Arabanoo grabbed Coorah's hand, and they raced with the others for the barricades of the first hill.

Coorah knew the scorpions were too strong, and too many. They were swarming toward the peak of the first hill, the only barrier between them and the eucalyptus forest. Then they'd pour into the Amphibilands without anything to stop them.

Chief Olba sounded another retreat, and there was nowhere to go except to the base of the first hill. So they did. And for a moment, the two armies faced each other, thousands of scorpions at the top of the hill, supported by grizzled lizards and silken spiders, and the bedraggled frogs waiting at the bottom for the final thrust.

For a long moment, a silence seemed to descend on the late afternoon. Coorah wiped her forehead and looked at the ragtag defenders. She saw Arabanoo in the front rank, bloody, with one eye swollen shut.

His other eye winked at her, and she smiled, though she wanted to cry.

Then the final attack began.

# 40

URSTING FROM THE EUCALYPTUS forest, Darel watched the scorpion army swarm down the first of the Outback Hills, crashing into the frog barricades.

He saw Captain Killara's lizards flanking the scorps on one side and a mass of spiders on the other. He caught a glimpse of Chief Olba in lily-pad armor swinging a club and Old Jir slashing with his cane from a hole in a log.

Darel's heart clenched when he saw Gee's parents kicking rocks at a knot of scorpions, their powerful legs working furiously—while his own mother opened a bag of stinging flies to swarm the scorpions.

Darel didn't even need to glance at Gee, who was hopping beside him. He felt him there, felt Gee's anger and determination as if it were his own.

Darel screamed, "*Kulipari!*" and, despite the heavy backpack, took the longest leap of his life.

He arced into the air. A rain of arrows shot past

him, and for a moment he thought that a regiment of enemy archers must've appeared behind him. Then he realized the arrows were all coming from Dingo.

She was standing on a boulder, her eyes black and her skin glowing a bright orange-red with black stripes. And her hands were a blur, a stream of arrows flying from her bow so fast that they looked like a single, endless arrow.

The spiders returned fire, but she danced effortlessly around their webs, shouting insults and felling scorpion after scorpion. She'd tapped into her poison. She'd transformed from an ordinary frog into something else.

Into a Kulipari.

And she wasn't the only one.

Burnu streaked forward, a blur of black and yellow-green, directly into the center of a seething mass of scorpion heavy infantry.

His boomerangs flashed and spun, and scorpions fell. He grabbed a scorp, rammed him into the ground, then sprang over him. He caught his boomerangs in the air and threw them again, landing with both feet on another enemy warrior.

Without any fanfare, Quoba quietly infiltrated a scorpion phalanx, and her staff blurred until the lead

scorpion realized she was alone. The scorp turned—and caught Quoba's staff across her head so hard that her carapace shattered and she fell in a lifeless heap.

Quoba seemed to melt into the ground, then reappeared beside a red-banded scorpion threatening Coorah and Arabanoo. She bashed two of his legs, leaving him for Coorah and Arabanoo to finish off. Darel smiled when she drifted toward Captain Killara and his lizards.

And Ponto?

Ponto was a glowing yellow-and-black scythe cutting a path through the thickest scorpion positions. Enemy soldiers flew like popcorn in the air above him. Then he grabbed two scorpions by the tail and hurled them at the spider archers.

Darel saw all of that in an instant, as he launched himself into the battle.

He landed on the largest of the scorpions threatening his mother and slammed him into a moaning heap. A second scorpion's stinger whipped toward him, but Gee smacked the attacker so hard with his stick that he flattened the two scorps behind him, too.

"You're alive!" his mother called, her eyes shining when she saw him.

Gee's dad shouted, "Gurnugan!"

"You are *so* ponded," Gee's mom said. "Where have you been? How did you—"

"We brought the Kulipari," Darel interrupted, adjusting his backpack. "They'll keep the scorp army busy while Gee and I . . ."

Darel's mom touched his face. "While you what?"

"While we end this," he told her.

He leaped into a nearby tree, clung with his toe pads, and shouted above the clamor of battle. "The Kulipari have returned! The Kulipari are *here*!"

"And we're giving the scorps free dance lessons," Dingo called, doing a handstand on top of a particularly evil-looking scorpion, then backflipping into the fray, dodging and laughing until ten scorpions were hot on her heels.

She led them directly into a tree trunk that Ponto was swinging like a bat. The wood cracked against the pursuing scorpions, and they were flung through the air over the battlefield.

"Run, little scorplings!" Burnu shouted, reaching behind himself to catch one of his returning boomerangs without even looking at it. "Run while you still can!"

He traded blows with an elite spider guard, then

spun away to dispatch an entire squad of scorpions. The spider guard's eyes glowed as he bared his fangs to plunge into Burnu's back—then they bulged even more when Burnu's other boomerang smacked him in the neck.

Quoba had disappeared in the melee near the lizards, and Darel smiled at her absence—and at the thrill that passed through the frog army when they realized they weren't alone.

Standing on the tree branch, Darel felt the eyes of hundreds of frogs on him. With the arrival of the Kulipari, a momentary hush seemed to fall over the battlefield. Darel filled his lungs and shouted, "You all know me, and you know I'm an ordinary frog. But I left the Amphibilands, I left the protection of the Veil—I walked into the heart of the scorpion camp, and look at me! I'm still alive. They're strong, but we're stronger. Wood frogs and tree frogs, burrowers and swimmers—we're stronger! They think they can steal our land? They think they can turn our forests into deserts? Not while *I* still breathe. I will fight them—and I will win. Who's with me?"

Across the battlefield, Coorah grabbed Arabanoo's hand. "We are!"

Arabanoo's tree frogs shouted, "And us!"

A great croaking arose from the hunters and trackers, from the farmers and merchants and crafters. "We are!"

Ponto roared his approval and tossed his tree into a snarl of scorpions. Frogs hopped through a break in the scorpion line, following Burnu and Dingo. With the Kulipari in front, the frog army drove the scorpions and spiders slowly uphill . . .

Until the spider queen's nightcasters started weaving their foul magic.

Spider silk fell in thick strands from the evening sky, spooling around the frogs, as strong as corded vine and as sticky as tree sap. The Kulipari sliced through the strands, but Darel noticed the warriors weren't glowing so brightly anymore. They were losing power.

He dodged an attacking spider and turned to Gee. "The Kulipari are going to burn out if they don't stop soon."

"Duck!" Gee croaked, and Darel dropped, narrowly avoiding a slashing pincer, then lashed out with one of his legs.

As the sticky silk continued to fall, the frog advance

slowed, then stopped. The Kulipari still blazed—but not as brilliantly—and the endless scorpion armies continued to pour into the Amphibilands.

With Gee at his side, Darel fought closer and closer to the lizard troops. He was finally in the thick of battle, but it wasn't like his daydreams. Real war was ugly, with pincers slashing and screams of pain. The stink of blood and terror filled his nostrils, and his body ached while his mind throbbed with worry.

Was his mom okay? How about Coorah and Old Jir and the triplets?

He swallowed his fear and pressed onward until a cry sounded from the frogs on the other side of the battlefield.

"What's that?" he asked.

Gee risked a glance in the direction of the sound. "King Sergu and Yabber are here! And their crocs."

Darel parried a scorpion tail, his dagger ringing against the stinger. He staggered, and the scorpion lunged—directly into a rock-trap the frogs had built earlier.

"Yabber's protecting the king," Gee reported, as they skirted a mass of spider warriors. "Oh, no.

Commander Pigo's after them. He's going to—
I can't look."

"What's the king doing?" Darel asked, slashing a
battle net with his dagger.

"He's dreamcasting, I think. Either that or
napping."

"He'd better stop this falling silk soon. Look at
the Kulipari. They don't have much time left; they're
exhausting their poison."

"The king's got more worries than that. Pigo's
surrounding him with those red-banded scorps."

"And *we*," a voice said, "are surrounding *you*."

Captain Killara and two dozen of his lizard mercenaries formed a ragged circle around Darel and Gee.

"You've got no chance against all of us," Killara
said, his tongue tasting the air. "Sheathe your weapon."

Darel sheathed his dagger, and Gee tossed his
stick aside. Then Killara snapped manacles around
their wrists and dragged them away. Toward the scorpion command post.

Toward Lord Marmoo.

# 41

COORAH GASPED WHEN THE FIRST strands of silk fell from the sky. She'd heard of nightcasting but never imagined she'd actually see such a terrible thing. In minutes, the tide of the battle turned. With every frog struggling under the sticky silk, the scorpions and spiders regained the upper hand.

Even the Kulipari, who had seemed invincible, were starting to slow down.

She remembered something Darel had told her: that Old Jir had been a Kulipari once, but he'd exhausted his powers and lost all his strength. Looking with the eyes of a healer, she could tell that these three—or four, she wasn't sure—new Kulipari were close to that point.

The arrival of the turtle king and his helper gave her hope. Except they didn't seem to join the battle so much as just . . . sit there.

Then the scariest of the scorpions cut through the

frog army, directly toward the turtles. Exhausted from the battle and the nightcast silk, the frogs fell back.

But not Coorah. She was treating a patient; she wouldn't retreat. And not Arabanoo and his tree frogs, either, forming a guard around her.

That's why they were close when it happened.

While Coorah splinted a broken bone, the turtle king suddenly opened his eyes. "It's done, Yabber. The Veil will stand, and I narrowed the rip that the spider queen tore. The frogs will need to defend only the Outback Hills, not every single border." His croc reared upward and slammed a few attacking scorpions. "Now I'll stop this rain of webbing. Jarrah's grown strong, it's true, but—"

"I already took care of it!" Yabber blurted, arching his long neck. "Look around! I'm telling you, Your Exalted Shelliness, I'm finally getting the hang of this dreamcasting business."

The old king peered upward. "Indeed you are. Jarrah's silk is faltering already . . . There. Stopped. Well done, my star pupil."

Coorah glanced at the sky: no more silken strands were falling from above. But now the scorpions had the turtles surrounded—not that they seemed very concerned.

"Oh, it's nothing," Yabber said, as his croc batted at the scorpions with his tail. "Not when you've learned from the best—which I have, of course. I mean you, Your Majestic Turtlehood, and I suppose that—"

"Yabber!" the king interrupted. "Pay attention. Is there anything we can do for the Kulipari? They're weakening."

"Well, I'm not sure if—"

At a signal from their commander, all of the red-banded scorpions sprang at the king's crocodile, pincers snapping and stingers curved.

"Watch out!" Coorah shouted.

The king's crocodile snapped and thrashed, but somehow the scorpion commander vaulted onto her back, directly behind Sergu.

And before Coorah could shout another warning, the scorpion commander drove his stinger into the king's unprotected neck.

The king gasped and collapsed in his saddle.

Yabber turned at the sound, his eyes round and terrified—then furious. A wave of power poured from him, flinging the scorps fifty feet in all directions: a raw explosion of force completely unlike ordinary dreamcasting.

And then, with her head still dizzy from the blast of

power, Coorah saw three things. She saw King Sergu slumped in his saddle—dying. She saw the Kulipari, their colors fading, facing battalions of fresh scorpion troops. And she saw Darel and Gee, manacled and defeated, being dragged by the lizards behind enemy lines.

# 42

ROM HIS COMMAND POST, MARMOO watched the lizard mercenaries dragging two young frogs closer. He hoped one of them was Darel, the croaker who'd infiltrated his camp. He clicked his mouthparts, savoring his victory over the young frog and his precious Amphibilands.

Temporarily allying himself with the spider queen had proved wise. Her nightcasting had drained the Kulipari.

He glanced at her, wondering if the time was right to strike.

"The turtle king!" she cried, her eyes shining.

"What?" he asked.

She laughed triumphantly. "Your Commander Pigo struck a killing blow. I can feel that King Sergu is dying. Look, there!"

In a clearing in the battle below them, two crocodiles snarled and snapped. And on the back of the larger croc, King Sergu slumped in a pathetic heap.

Marmoo scanned the battlefield for Pigo and raised his pincer to summon him, then told Jarrah, "Do you see what my promises are worth? I told you I'd give you the turtle, and here he is, dying at your feet. Now, then—what happened to your webs, the ones falling from the sky?"

"My ladies-in-waiting are handling that. They..." Jarrah frowned, confusion hardening her expression. "They stopped casting. Something's wrong."

Stepping out of the command post, Marmoo looked toward the ladies-in-waiting and for a moment didn't understand what he was seeing. Seven big bundles of silk lay on the ground. The ladies-in-waiting were nowhere to be seen.

Except ... those bundles *were* the ladies-in-waiting. As if the magic had turned on them and consumed them.

"What is this?" Jarrah snarled beside him.

"The turtle king! He did this." She stalked toward the bundles. "No, not *him*. That bumbling apprentice—he killed my ladies. I'll tear out his eyes and use his shell as a table, I'll . . ."

Marmoo turned away, hiding a smirk. He was pleased with the results of his alliance with the spider queen but even more pleased to see the limits of her powers. Now that the Amphibilands had fallen, it was only a matter of time until he got rid of Jarrah.

## 43

WITH A HEAVY BACKPACK slung over one scaly shoulder, Captain Killara dragged Darel along the uneven ground.

Rocks scraped at the frog as he struggled weakly against his manacles. He turned his face away from the jeering crowds of scorpion warriors, his heart beating fast.

Beside him, Gee squirmed. "Let go, snakeface!"

Nogo the rock lizard smacked Gee with a scaly paw, then hauled him closer to Lord Marmoo's command post.

Finally, Killara tossed Darel to the ground.

Darel grunted at the impact and rose into a crouch, his manacled hands in front of him. He took a look at Marmoo. There was no question why he was the scorpion lord. With his carapace gleaming and his jointed tail swiveling above him, he was so commanding that he made even the brutal Pigo, who stood next to him, look harmless.

"*This* is the frog who defied me?" Marmoo said as he eyed Darel disdainfully. "This little nothing of a mud-belly?"

"That's right," Darel said, swallowing his nervousness. "I guess that means you're pretty easy to defy."

Marmoo leaned closer, his tail curving overhead. "The Amphibilands is mine. I'll crush your burrows and eat your tadpoles. You have brothers and sisters? Commander Pigo likes them raw. Isn't that right, Pigo?"

"Yes, my lord."

"I prefer them roasted on a skewer, myself." Marmoo's mouthparts shifted in anticipation. "There's no accounting for taste."

Darel gulped. "You'll never take the Amphibilands."

"I already have."

"You haven't even gotten past *me*."

"Past you, little frogling?" Marmoo sneered. "You're not an obstacle—you're a snack. After I sting you, I'll use your hide to polish my tail."

Darel almost smiled at the word "sting." Instead, he puffed his throat. "You're not fast enough to sting me."

Marmoo's side eyes narrowed, and he leaned closer, looming above the crouching, manacled Darel. "The turtle king's dying," he snarled. "The Kulipari are tapped out. I'm going to kill everything you love, croaker—every pond, every tree, every friend and family member."

"You'll try," Darel said.

Marmoo reared back to strike. He was so close that Darel saw his pale underbelly stretched above him, saw his tail quiver and his stinger flash downward.

A moment before impact, Darel slipped his hands from the unlocked manacles. At the same moment, Gee shot his tongue out, even faster than a scorpion's sting, and snagged Marmoo's tail.

That was all the time Darel needed.

He dove forward, under Marmoo. The scorpion lord's tail whipped forward again, but Darel was quicker. He plunged his dagger deep into Marmoo's unprotected belly.

Marmoo bellowed in anger and pain, then toppled to his side—and all the scorpions nearby froze, staring in confusion and disbelief at their fallen lord.

By the time Pigo remembered himself and started screaming orders, Darel and Gee had sprung into the air, leaping into the thick of the lizard mercenaries.

They raced past Killara, who blocked the scorpions' pursuit. The lizard captain still wore Darel's back-pack—which was full of the turtle king's sand dollars.

Darel heard Pigo behind him, shouting, "Betrayed! We've been betrayed by the lizards!"

"You only paid us to *enter* the Amphibilands," Killara answered. "We accepted a new client for the rest of the day. Happy to serve you again tomorrow, though, Commander Pigo."

Darel laughed as he bounded away.

That had been his plan: Quoba had ghosted across enemy lines and offered Killara the turtle king's money to pretend to capture Darel and Gee . . . and to leave their manacles unlocked. Killara resented the scor-pions for underpaying him and was willing to work for Darel instead.

After all of his dreams of battlefield triumph, Darel had used old-fashioned wood-frog cunning to win.

"Now what?" Gee asked, as they landed in the branches of an acacia tree.

"Now Pigo will retreat," Darel said. "Scorpions don't fight once their leader's down."

Gee puffed out his throat. "That's the only *good* thing about scorps."

"That and their soft underbelly."

"I can't believe you killed Marmoo," Gee said, his eyes bulging. "That's just . . . wow! I mean—Darel, you *killed* Marmoo!"

"Well, I had a little help from a friend."

Gee grinned for a second, then looked nervous. "But the spider queen's still alive. And you know she's already planning on coming back."

"Not today, though," Darel told him. "Today, we won."

And as he said the words, the scorpions sounded a retreat, then scuttled away.

## 44

AREL!" A FAMILIAR VOICE CALLED.

Darel looked away from the re-treating scorpion hordes. "Coorah! You're all right! I was—"

"Come quickly! King Sergu is asking for you. There's not much time."

Darel hopped with Coorah across the battlefield toward the two crocodiles. Standing nearby were Chief Olba and the Kulipari and Yabber.

The turtle king rested on a stretcher. Coorah's father was treating him . . . but he looked pretty bad. Actually, he looked dead. His eyes were closed, and he didn't seem to be breathing.

Then Coorah leaped into action. She pulled poultices from her pouch and croaked instructions to her father, telling him to mix three herbs into a paste. She inspected the king's wounded neck, and her fingers were a blur as she started treating him.

A minute later, the turtle king took a shallow breath, and then his eyelids flickered.

"You did it, Coorah," Gee said, his voice awed. "You saved him!"

Coorah shook her head. "No, the poison's too deep. I—I'm sorry. He doesn't have long."

"You did well, healer," King Sergu whispered. "You've given me a chance to say . . . one last thing."

Darel felt his eyes moisten and blinked away his tears.

"Come closer, everyone," King Sergu said, weakly. "You too, Darel." He took a shallow breath. "Soon the battle will begin again. And the next time, I won't be here to fight alongside you."

"What shall we do?" Chief Olba asked.

"Protect yourselves," the dying king said. "You have the Kulipari now, and Yabber."

"I'm just an apprentice!" Yabber said. "I don't know how to—"

The king raised his flipper, and Yabber fell silent. "And the Amphibilands has a secret weapon," Sergu continued.

"So secret that even *I* don't know what it is?" Chief Olba said.

"Not *what*," the king answered, with a weak smile. "*Who*. There is more strength in ordinary frogs than anyone knows. You don't need poison to become heroes. Darel proved that."

"That's our secret weapon?" Olba asked. "Frogs?"

"One of you must lead the defense," the turtle king said. "One of you must teach these farmers and merchants how to fight for their homes. Must train warriors and—"

"Always willing to serve, my king," Burnu said, with a crisp salute. "I will command the defense and train the frogs. I will—"

"He doesn't mean you," Quoba said, in her soft voice.

"No," the king said. He pointed shakily at Darel. "I mean *you.*"

"Me?" Darel croaked. He'd always imagined that victory would mean applause and a big medal, not more responsibility. "But I don't know the first thing about defending the Amphibilands."

"You will learn," Sergu whispered, a faint smile on his creased face. "The Kulipari aren't the only frogs with power."

"They're the only ones with *poison*, though."

"Ordinary frogs don't need poison," the king repeated, his golden eyes closing. "You will learn to tap the power that is already inside you. You will . . ."

The turtle king died with the rest of his words unspoken.

# ≼ 45 ≽

HEY BURIED KING SERGU AND the fallen soldiers with honors. A mournful chorus sang, and Chief Olba gave a speech of tribute. In the crowd, curious children clustered around Yabber and the Kulipari. Gee's brother Miro perched on one of Ponto's massive shoulders, and a young tree frog sat on the other.

Afterward, in the tradition of the Amphibilands, a feast was served between the meadow and the nursery pond.

Tadpoles splashed through the water, chasing Dingo and trying to mimic her impossible acrobatics. Coorah sat with a much-bandaged Arabanoo amid a profusion of flowers, gifts from the dozens of frogs she'd saved. Burnu stood behind Chief Olba, strong and fierce. Quoba was nowhere to be seen—as usual.

Darel and Gee sat at a round table with their parents, nibbling on sweetcakes and moss flowers.

"Get another plate, Gurnugan," Gee's dad said. "You're all skin and bones."

"I wouldn't go *that* far," his mother said.

"You should've seen him attack the scorpion lord," Darel said. "Gee's all muscle and gristle. With maybe a *tiny* layer of insulation."

Everyone laughed. After snatching a last sugar-fly from the bowl with his tongue, Darel leaned back in his seat, and his mother put her hand on his arm. She didn't say anything, but he saw the pride in her eyes.

Then Chief Olba stood from her chair and called, "Darel! Where's Darel? Oh, there you are. Stand up, son."

Darel stood, his nostrils narrowing in embarrassment when everyone looked at him.

"We're here today," Olba said, "because of one stubborn young frog who refused to quit. The Amphibilands is safe because of him. When Darel—" The rest of her words were lost in applause and whistles. Finally, when the crowd quieted, she said, "Care to say a few words, Darel?"

He took a deep breath. "Before the turtle king died, he said that the Amphibilands has a secret weapon." Darel looked into the crowd. "*Us.* Ordinary

frogs. There's still a rip in the Veil, and one day soon our enemies will attack again. But we can stand against them if we stand together. In this fight, we're *all* Kuli-pari."

A croaking cheer rose above the village, above the nursery pool and the banyan tree. It echoed from the coast to the hills, and Darel caught Gee's eye and smiled.

# 46

EEP IN THE OUTBACK, A JAGGED black plateau rose from the desert. Spiders and scorpions swarmed over the nearby dunes, and Commander Pigo paced anxiously among them, his mouthparts drawn into a worried frown.

Far above, in the moonlight, Queen Jarrah circled a shimmering white shape on the top of the plateau. She wrapped it tighter in her web, then paused and eyed the silken cocoon.

It was larger than the spider herself, a huge mass of glossy webbing. And completely motionless . . . for now.

Jarrah extended her fangs. Poison glistened on the needle-sharp tips, then dropped onto strands of silk that she had wrapped around the cocoon. She started nightcasting, and her eyes turned completely black. The night air shimmered with power.

Then, in a flash, she sank her fangs into the silken

cocoon, pumping poison through the webbing until she had nothing left. She staggered backward, weak and exhausted, and stood with her head bowed as a chill breeze whipped around her.

The cocoon twitched. The silk rippled and bulged. Then a dark rip tore down one side. A moment later, a glossy black pincer appeared through the rip.

A scorpion claw.

# ABOUT THE AUTHORS AND ILLUSTRATOR

**T**REVOR PRYCE is a retired NFL player and writer who's written for the *New York Times* and NBC.com. He's also developed television and movie scripts for Sony Pictures, Cartoon Network, Disney, ABC, and HBO, among others. He lives in Maryland.

**J**OEL NAFTALI is the author of many books, several written with his wife, Lee. He lives in California.

**S**ANFORD GREENE is an accomplished comics illustrator whose work has been published by DC Comics, Disney, Nickelodeon, Dark Horse, and more. He lives in South Carolina.

EEP IN HER SNUG BURROW, Okipippi woke early—which for a platypus meant "before sunset"—and yawned and stretched. She drowsed in her comfy twig nest for a few minutes, listening to her parents snoring away in the other room.

Then she rubbed her eyes and noticed that her sister's nest was empty. Pirra was probably already on the river, floating around with her friends. Pippi wasn't old enough to swim in the river before dark, but that didn't bother her. She liked to spend most of her time with the Stargazer anyway.

The platypus tribe didn't have a chief or a king or a queen. If they needed advice, they went to the Stargazer, an old gray-furred platypus with notched ears and bright eyes. She taught the newborn pups after they hatched in the deep, mud-walled nurseries, and she had her own kind of magic. Not dreamcasting, like the turtles. Not nightcasting, like the spiders. The

Stargazer simply twirled herself into a trance, then focused on the distant whispering of the Rainbow Serpent, the ancient god who'd brought life to the Australian outback.

Pippi loved the legends of the Rainbow Serpent. She liked the one about the colors of the Serpent dripping onto the Kulipari to give them power, and the one about her great-great-grandparents digging endless burrows beneath the outback—tunnels that connected the deep waters of the Amphibilands to the rest of the land.

But her favorite story explained how the Serpent had created the platypus in its own image. Just as a rainbow contained many different colors, a platypus contained many different parts: a duck-like bill; webbed feet; thick, waterproof fur; and a chunky tail. The males even had a poison spur on one ankle!

Maybe that's why the platypuses followed the Serpent more closely than anyone else. At least, the Stargazer did. She didn't actually *talk* to the Rainbow Serpent, but she deciphered messages in the ripples and splashes of the river's current. There were a hundred myths and tales and legends about the Serpent, but they all agreed that the ancient water god had breathed life into a dry land, creating streams and lakes and pools.

After one final yawn, Pippi wandered into the kitchen, grabbed a crayfish tail, and called, "Mom! Dad! I'm going outside!"

"Don't go too far," came her father's sleepy voice. "You're still a platypup."

"Okay!" she called back as she headed for the burrow entrance.

Old trees rose along the wide river that snaked through the platypus village, and their roots twined down along the riverbank—some gnarled and thick, others as skinny as kite strings. Most of the village burrows were hidden behind the curtain of roots, dozens of neat holes just above the waterline.

Using her wide webbed foot, Pippi pushed aside the dangling roots. She looked at the blue water shifting to gray in the fading light of day. Furry brown platypuses floated lazily in the river, getting ready to hunt, their duck-bills breaking the surface and their beaver-like tails swishing behind them.

Pippi spotted her sister. But since Pippi was too young to slip into the water until the safety of nightfall, she stayed where she was and ate the last bite of crayfish tail. Then she climbed the riverbank, walking on her knuckles to protect the sensitive webbing between her toes. Most platypuses didn't like walking on dry land, but Pippi didn't mind. Pirra called her a weirdo and their parents called her a dreamer, but the Stargazer just said that she was curious.

She headed upstream, toward the gentle roar of the rapids. Mist drifted through the air, and she paused now and then to lick the moisture from her fur. Walking on dry land made her thirsty.

Finally, she stopped beneath a riberry tree that grew from the bank of the river. Roots dangled over a wide burrow mouth, and she parted them with her bill.

"Stargazer?" she called. "Are you awake?"

"Hmm . . . I *think* so," the Stargazer's soft voice said from within. "But what if I'm asleep, and dreaming that I'm awake?"

Pippi giggled. "Then you wouldn't be talking to me!"

"Come in, Pippi," the Stargazer said with a laugh. "I'm in the dripping room."

Pippi waddled deeper into a comfy curving tunnel that ballooned here and there into a kitchen, living room, and bedrooms. It looked like everyone else's burrow, except the Stargazer also had a "dripping room"—a candlelit earthen chamber with one wall of solid rock. Water trickled down the wall, making damp, crisscrossing tracks and splatters.

Pippi found the Stargazer staring at the wall. The elderly platypus's small eyes were bright in the flickering light.

"I feel the call of the Rainbow Serpent," the Stargazer told her. "An important message, but I can't quite make it out."

Pippi settled beside her and squinted at the wall.

"What do you see?" the Stargazer asked.

"Um . . . mostly rock," Pippi answered. "And some water."

The Stargazer *tsk*ed. "Look closer. The Rainbow Serpent speaks to us through water."

Pippi wrinkled her bill and peered intently at the wall.

Water dripped. Patches of moisture caught the glint of the candles. The roar of the rapids outside sounded like a thousand platypuses murmuring. The damp tracks of the water seemed almost to form a picture, a mural, a—

The Stargazer gasped. "There! Did you see?"

"What? Where?" Pippi blinked. *Had* she seen something? "I'm not sure."

"I'm afraid . . ." The Stargazer stepped closer to the wall and, for a long moment, just studied the dripping water. Then she rubbed her face and sighed. "I'm afraid it's bad news, Pippi—indeed, the worst I've seen."

Pippi shifted nervously. "What's wrong?"

"We're in danger, the whole tribe."

"F–f–from what?"

"I think . . . birds? It's not clear. But something in the air."

"When—now? I'll run and tell everyone!"

"Wait. It's not just us. The whole outback is under threat—all the wet places, all the streams and springs." The Stargazer swayed as her eyes became unfocused. "A war is coming . . . a battle for water. The final battle. The scorpions and spiders and—"

"*They* can't hurt us!" Pippi said, her voice squeaking. "Everyone knows bugs can't swim. We can hide in the river if they come."

"But the spider queen knows that we listen to the Rainbow Serpent, and she knows the Serpent will oppose her. She'll try to kill us, to silence the Serpent—nobody else heeds the signs the way we do. I see villages burned, Pippi. Death and destruction and wetlands turned into desert . . ."

Pippi's bill trembled in fear. "Wh-wh-what should I do?"

"We need help. We need the Blue Sky King."

"The what?"

"The frog called Darel," the Stargazer told her. "From the Amphibilands."

"Th-th-the one who beat the scorpion lord?"

The Stargazer nodded. "He is the key."

"Blue Sky King?" Pippi blinked in confusion. "Isn't he more of a Brown Pond Prince?"

The Stargazer smiled but didn't explain. Instead, she fell into a trance, humming to herself and shuffling from side to side as she gazed at the droplets of water on the rock wall.

"Stargazer?" Pippi said. But the old platypus was already lost in her dreaming.

Pippi knew better than to disturb her. With her heart pounding, she raced toward home. A war for water? The final war? Entire villages destroyed? A *frog*?

When she reached the village, she paused on a mossy log above the river to catch her breath. She spotted Pirra lazing in the current, but before Pippi could call out, a look of concern crossed her sister's face.

Turning to a friend floating nearby, Pirra asked, "What's that? Do you feel that?"

"Is it a shrimp?" her friend said, shaking his head slowly. Platypuses had a special sense beyond sight and smell and hearing—when they moved their bills back and forth, they could pick up electric fields created by other animals. "Water worms? I'm not feeling a tingle."

"I can't tell," Pirra said. "It's almost like it's coming from above."

Pippi spun to peer through the dusk, her fear suddenly as sharp as a blade.

"Worms can't fly," the friend cracked. "You're getting as weird as your sister."

"Okipippi isn't weird!" Pirra could call Pippi that, but no one else could. "She's just . . . little."

Pippi almost smiled, happy that her sister had defended her, even if she had called her "little." Then she spotted motion in the trees: a flurry of white wings swooping and darting silently toward the river.

What *was* that? Not birds. Not fireflies. Then she realized, staring in shock. Bats! *Ghost bats!* She knew that the village sometimes fought the bats, if two hunting parties stumbled into each other in the middle of the night. But not like this—not an entire war party attacking the village for no reason.

"Bats!" she screamed. "Bats are coming!"

Pirra swiveled in the water, finally seeing her. "Quiet, Pippi! You're going to wake the—"

"Ghost bats!" Pippi yelled, pointing frantically into the woods. "They're coming!"

"And now," the friend said with a snort, "she believes in ghosts. She's such a—" He stopped when he saw the bats emerging from the trees, then screamed, "Bats! Help! Bats!"

As other young platypuses started yelling, the grown-ups sleepily emerged from the root-hidden burrows along the riverbank. At first they grumbled at the noise, but then they saw the bats angling directly toward them.

"Watch out!" Pippi yelled. "Go back!"

It was too late. The ghost bats, their needle-sharp fangs bared, streamed through the air toward the slower-moving platypuses. A chubby platypus swiped at a bat with the poison spur on his back foot, but the bat simply flitted backward, higher in the air. A moment later, a gang of bats attacked the chubby platypus, teeth slashing. Pippi looked away in horror.

"Get inside quickly!" Pirra yelled. "Everyone, block off your burrows! Pippi, c'mon!"

Pippi started to slide down the muddy bank to the safety of the water, but three white bats, fangs glistening, suddenly appeared in front of her.

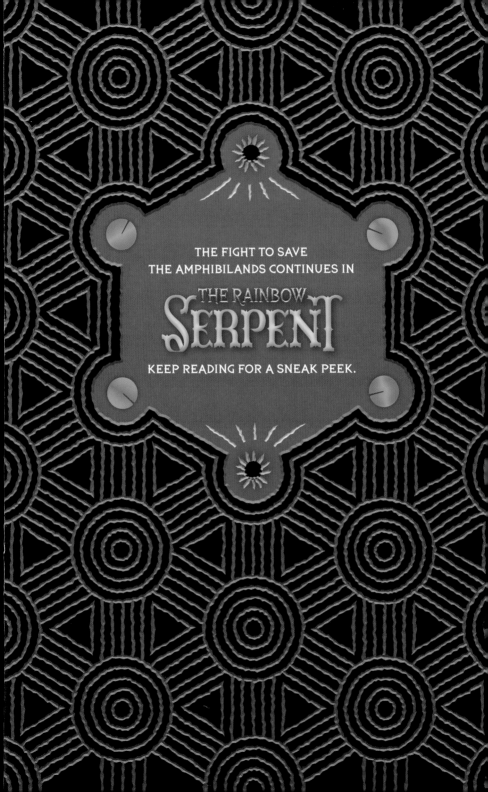

THE FIGHT TO SAVE
THE AMPHIBILANDS CONTINUES IN

# THE RAINBOW
# SERPENT

KEEP READING FOR A SNEAK PEEK.